D0989147

GREAT BALLS OF FIRE!

Harry Harrison

First published in Great Britain in 1977
Pierrot Publishing Limited, London

Library of Congress catalog card number: 77-79649
ISBN 0-448-14377-1 (hardcover edition)
ISBN 0-448-14378-X (paperback edition)

First Grosset & Dunlap edition 1977

Printed and bound in Italy by Mohn Gordon.

Contents

1

The Sex Queen of Outer Space

Early science fiction illustrations always promised more than the text delivered—as least as far as the sex went. Yes, the giant rockets really were in the stories, as depicted on the cover, as well as the riveted robots and scintillating rays of unknown colors that could slice solid steel as though it were soft butter. Plenty of delivery of promise in these areas, satisfying every spotty little boy's desire to rocket away through the galaxy. But where was the girl in the brazen brassière about to be eaten—or worse!—by the tentacled monster? Nowhere in the magazine, buddy, not in that time and era.

It was the early 1930's and the Depression was grinding joy into very small bits. University graduates went directly from school to the breadline and the world was an unrelieved gray. Well, *almost* unrelieved. The Sunday newspapers, full standard size, were big as bedsheets and crackled with color. You could have a laugh with *Bringing Up Father*, shed a tear with *Little Orphan Annie*, then explore the wonders of the distant world of Mongo with *Flash Gordon*. And all pure as new-fallen snow, you betcha. These newspapers went into homes right across the United States, and any teeny hint of smut would start the letters winging towards the publishers. Newspaper syndicate editors are the biggest cowards in the world. With millions of newspapers being published daily, they still cringe at a single letter from Mom in the Bible Belt. Snakes look like a you-know-what, so no snakes in the strips. Drinking is a sin—therefore the good guys can't drink. Year by year the list of forbidden objects grew longer and the newspaper comics grew cleaner. In those bygone days only *Flash Gordon*, drawn with great skill by Alex Raymond, would dare show a length of bared leg, a full, yet tastefully draped, bosom. There seemed to be a greater license on the alien worlds of SF for girls to rush about half-draped; Joe Palooka's girl-friend, Anne Howe—despite the despicable pun of her name—never lifted a hemline nor bared a cleavage for her punchy partner. Science fiction, the world "out there" was allowed certain greater freedoms, just as the travelogues and *National Geographic* could show naked black breasts in the depths of darkest Africa.

The more garish of the science fiction magazines took advantage of this unspoken liberality and flaunted flimsily clad girls in the grip of things or machines, obviously bent on interspecies or mechanistic rape. Good stuff! No wonder our parents threw these magazines into the garbage can when they found them. *Their* lives contained no such colorful pleasures. We could escape and they could not. This was the joy of science fiction, then—and hopefully now.

That wily old Luxembourger magazine publishing fiend, Hugo Gernsback, started the whole thing. Not happy with such titles as *Radio Listener's Guide* and *Money Making*, he launched *Amazing Stories* in 1927. At first this kind of story was called scientifiction, later changed, thankfully, to science fiction. The field was launched, the category declared, the imitators followed—and science fiction fell upon an unsuspecting world.

Looking back through the telescope of time we, in our more liberal age, can only marvel at the naïveté of it all. SF was not only written for boys, it was *about* boys—thick-thewed and apparently as grown-up as they pretended to be. It was commonplace to have the nubile heroine stranded on a distant planet for years with the hero, and perhaps some chums, and emerge from this adventure with virginity not only intact but unremarked. The heroes, read boys, were far more interested in repairing the kronx drive of their spacer with bits of wire, or digging flonxite from the native rock to fuel the engine.

This was definitely not true of the boys reading the stuff. A lot of SF enthusiasts were precocious and began absorbing their favorite fiction at the age of seven or eight. So giant machines and horrifying alien monsters satisfied quite well for a number of years. But sooner or later puberty had to strike and a new interest entered life. Girls. Damned inaccessible in the flesh; copping a feel in the playground yard was about all the heterosexuality a city boy was capable of. But what about literature? If not the tit, then how about the titillation? Very little of it indeed; just the visual promise without the fictional follow-up. The only exception to this very firm rule was the "dirty book". These might be called the very first comic books for they were certainly circulated clandestinely in school toilets long before the first ten-cent comic hit the news-stands in 1934.

Dirty books were hideously drawn, badly printed and fantastically overpriced—anywhere from two-bits to a dollar for something that couldn't have cost a quarter of a cent to produce. They had thin cardboard covers with eight interior pages and were the size and shape of a small file card. They had standard comic strip titles but, oh, were they different inside.

Here was *Toots and Casper* with Casper sporting a weapon the size of a baseball bat—and actually working his oversized sexual will upon Toots. Great stuff! Made even more interesting by the fact that all of these shenanigans were taking place in what appeared to be a flasher's paradise. Since the cretinous artists who did these things could barely draw, the male characters all wore hats, helmets, leather jackets, etc. so they could be recognized. The girls managed to lose their clothes rather quickly, but there was Dick Tracy hard on the job nattily attired from the waist up—snap-brim hat and all.

Promises! Promises! But the dress never opened further, the bra strap could very well have been glued to the skin. Excitation without satisfaction was the name of the game.

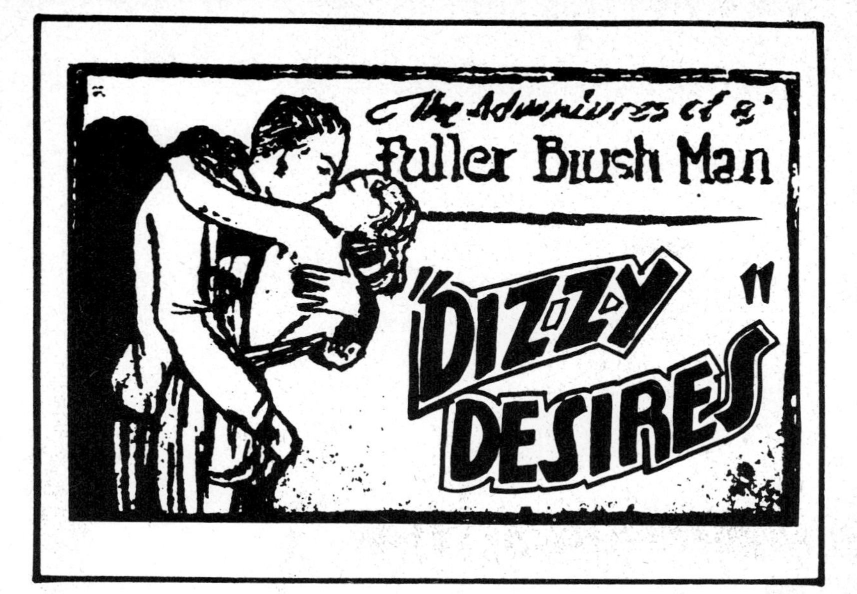

Do these badly drawn fantasies still exist? Are small boys still forking over their pocket-money for the illicit thrill of these wanking wonders? It is hard to believe. Gresham must surely be right, with porn as with money; today's hardcore porn in films, books and magazines, the really-rough, must surely have driven out the simply-dirty.

But dirty books were a luxury rarely afforded, and sure death for the owner if parent or teacher found them on a victim. Nor did they satisfy. Pulp magazines were the real escape, the true joy, and best of them all was science fiction. Here, in the depths of the galaxy, the burning drives of pubescence could be sublimated—at least for a little while.

Eventually, it had to come; slightly sexier pulps began to appear. It is to blush to apply the word "sexy" to them—but they sure looked good back in the late thirties when they first came out. Under the counter stuff, that is sold from a secret cache by the perverted newsie, not displayed on the racks with the rest of the magazines. Wild items with titles like *Spicy Mystery* and *Spicy Western Stories*. But best of all was *Spicy Adventure Stories* because this contained spicy science fiction—and this was true joy. It even contained spicy comics featuring dear old Diana Daw who was always losing her clothes on strange planets.

The stories were even better than the art because the guys actually *touched* the girls. Witness this inflaming scene from *Space Burial* by pseudonymous Lew Merrill.

> *Her lips met his with crushing pressure,*
> *and the roundness of her breasts became*
> *a broken bar across his chest.*

The simile is a little confusing, not to say uncomfortable, but there was better to come on the next page.

> *Astra snuggled up beside him. She had*
> *put off her robe in the hot compartment*
> *and she was a nectarine girl, for whom life*
> *meant love. In the circle of her arms,*
> *and dazed by her shimmering undergarment,*
> *Bill was lost again.*
> *Hours passed. Day and night followed*
> *each other at brief intervals ...*

That was all you got. Broken bar breasts and dazing shimmering undergarments. Not much, but far better than what had been coming along in the years before. Science fiction never again reached these easily scalable heights until a decade had passed. A war had to intervene before a revolution in mores penetrated these blood-drenched yet sexually pristine fields.

In order to appreciate the absence of sex in this type of fiction it should always be remembered what "category fiction" actually meant—in the magazine sense, not the modern publishing label. Category today is purely a book affair, a way of marketing and reaching an audience. Mystery readers read mysteries; science fiction fans buy SF. This may be tautological and obvious, but it is also still true. Publishers know all about it and writers learn about it slowly, usually the

Now, in the freer 70's, Diana Daw's granddaughter is much freer in displaying her body than grandma ever was. Not to mention being much better drawn! Even the SF hardware is more realistic, certainly a bit better than Diana's rock-plugged rocket. Perhaps being French helps.

hard way with a kick in the wallet. A category writer, who may sell 8,000 copies of his novels in hardcover, will discover that when one of his books is labelled mainstream, usually despite the pained screams of his editor, that it sells 345 copies.

This categorizing of fiction may have come out of the pulp magazines; if so it is one more burden of responsibility they must carry. Because in their heyday they sold monthly—even weekly—by the millions and categories and subcategories proliferated like rabbits. Before becoming a magazine category in its own right science fiction rattled around in a sidewater of the mainstream sometimes labelled scientific romances, sometimes not distinguished at all from the ordinary novel or short story. General fiction magazines at the end of the nineteenth century and into the twentieth printed SF along with all other kinds of fiction. Then along came Hugo Gernsback who liked to make money at publishing—but who also liked the role of a science teacher. The *Electrical Experimenter* lived up to its name with easy experiments at home, like electrocuting the cat. In case the articles did not carry the message that science was fun, there were fictional pieces that drove home this message.

And that was how it all began. During this period dozens of subdivided categories were born, waxed, waned—then died. SF is one of the few survivors. Only in crumbling and overpriced magazines, pulp collectors' items, will we ever see fiction magazines devoted solely to sea stories, weird stories, war stories, oriental tales, baseball players, cowboys—and what must be the most sickening subcategory of all time, the range romance. (An old-time pulp editor, who should know, swears that General Eisenhower was not a western story fan as is mooted about, but in reality was a devotee of the rangeland romance. If so, this explains a lot about his insecure grasp of English grammar.)

When early science fiction is considered solely as a product of the pulp jungle its restraints and limitations become obvious. Once Gernsback had exhausted Wells, Verne and Poe, as well as his own translations of French and German writers whose work fitted the new category, he had to look for new authors. He did not have to look very far because the pulp writers were already beating feebly on his door with their undernourished, ink-stained hands. These were the Good Old Hacks, the spiritual descendants of Grub Street, the cent-, or even half-cent-, a-word writers. It was a short

But in science fiction, as in life, maturity has to arrive, distasteful as it may appear to the pre-pubescent. Clothes can drop away—it takes but a stroke of the artist's pen—and the untouched creamy flesh can feel the caress of a man's hand at last. But not all clichés die that easily: men still have darker skins than girls.

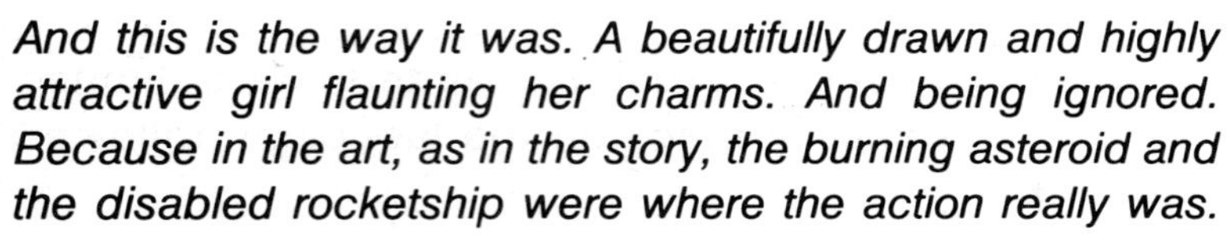

And this is the way it was. A beautifully drawn and highly attractive girl flaunting her charms. And being ignored. Because in the art, as in the story, the burning asteroid and the disabled rocketship were where the action really was.

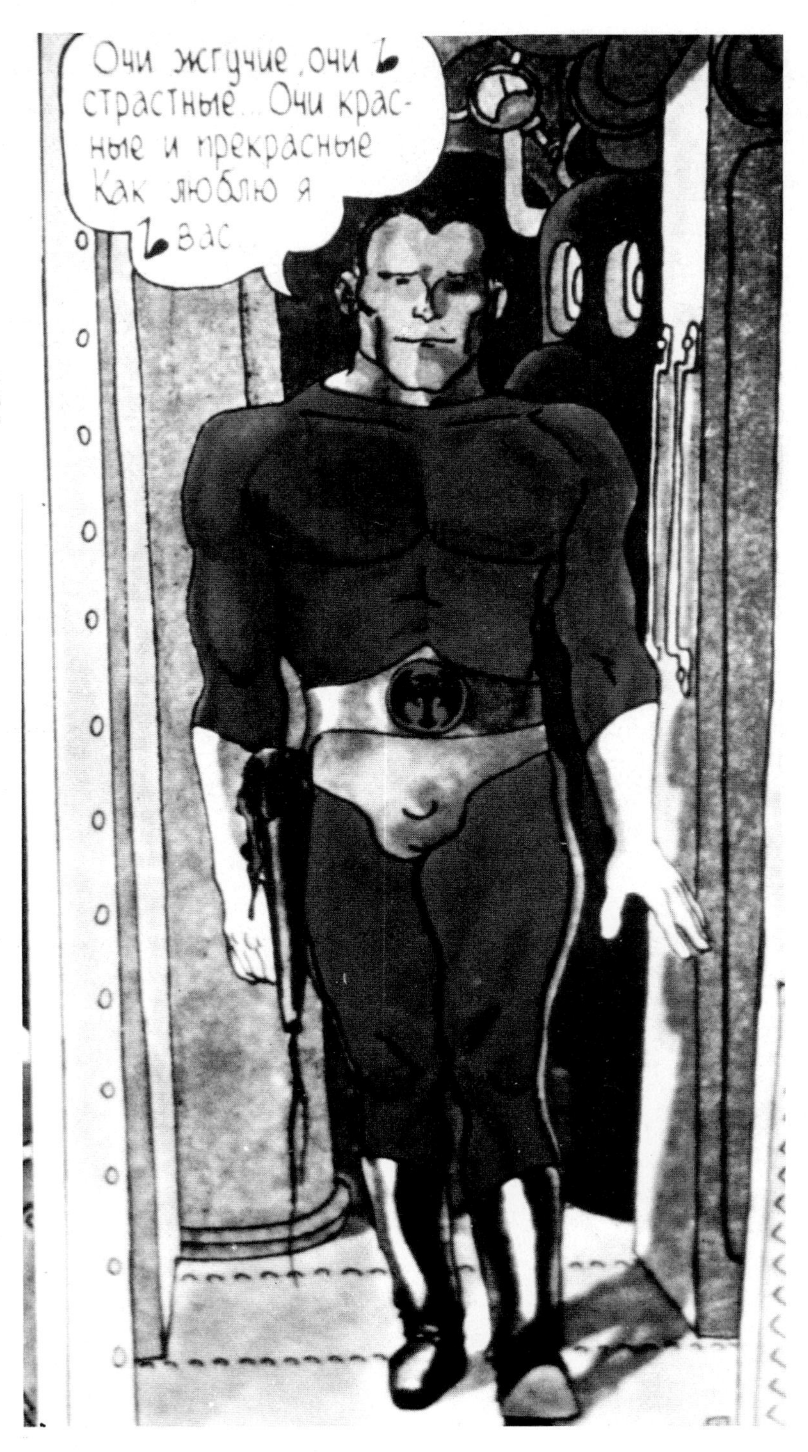

The modern spaceman not only gets the girl but he also has all the right bulges and a sense of humor—Russian too!

story in a day for them, a novelette tomorrow morning and a novel by Friday. They were not good—but they were sure fast. To understand the morality of their science fiction we must understand the morality of all popular pulp fiction of the time.

They had unwritten rules that they adhered to quite closely. Americans, and sometimes Englishmen, were good; all other foreigners, and particularly yellow ones, were bad. The Yellow Peril was the stock enemy and there was even one pulp magazine, *Operator Number 5*, which was devoted solely to battling this slant-eyed menace.

Violence and killing were okay as long as the hero did it cleanly and swiftly, and then only to the villains with strange names. The villains however were not above a bit of torture, the hot poker deftly placed and the chilling crack of the whip. Of course they were killed for this, so justice was seen to be served.

Sex did not exist; the only apparent reason for two sexes was so that there could be different names on toilet doors. (Not that toilets could be mentioned either.) Children were issued in various sizes to fit story needs, and entered and exited without being born or growing up. Women were either beautiful and young, to be rescued, or old and haggy to mutter warnings or sell newspapers from the corner stand. The reasons for all those attractive bumps and things that girls had was never stated, but could be hinted at indirectly. The young ladies were always kidnapped by the baddies for unstated reasons, but they had to be rescued instantly before something awful happened. There were no clues given why; they could have gone off like fish for all the reader knew. Heterosexual encounters were limited only to a kiss and embrace on the last page, followed by a quick fade.

Bad men drank, usually directly from a bottle labeled XXX, and did even worse things than normal while in their cups. Heroes did not drink but, in those pre-carcinogenous days, they did smoke like furnaces. This made for great display of silver cigarette cases which always helped move the story along.

Marijuana was unheard of, ''bennies'' hadn't been invented, and ''uppers and downers'' must have been elevator operators. Sherlock Holmes had taken cocaine, but the drug had never been heard of since. Evil orientals (see Yellow Peril) were often seen slipping into and out of opium dens, but no clue was ever given as to what occurred once the heavy door thudded shut.

Black men had thick lips, said ''yassuh, boss'' and made good, but unreliable, servants.

Red Indians were there to be shot.

It was a simple and simplistic world. Science fiction was born in it and still has not emerged completely. Therefore it is a great tribute to the strength and staying power of libidinous drives that sex did manage to wriggle into the picture from time to time.

Always the threat—and never the realization. At least not on the cover. While modern SF art does occasionally have the monster doing nasty things to the girl, or vice versa, this was never true in the good old days. What you saw was what you got; there was no follow-through inside the magazine. The girl, well-built but chastely draped, including gloves, shrank away and screamed while the hero defended her. Femlib still hasn't busted this field; the same routine continues with just a bit more flesh showing.

2

Early Promise

You did not have to be schizoid to read the early science fiction magazines—but it would have helped. The illustrations told one story, the words another. While the interior artwork occasionally had some connection with the stories they were illustrating, the covers rarely, if ever, had anything to do with the contents of the magazine—once the girls started being shown on them. In the beginning the hardware was what counted and if a girl appeared in the scene she was just there as a bystander or female friend of the hero who did all the work.

There is a gentleness in these first depictions of the female-form-divine that has since vanished from illustration—if not from the world. The sweet young things were daughters of the Gibson Girls, those svelte, controlled, tightly-buttoned maidens of Charles Dana Gibson. One of them even graced the contents page of *Wonder Stories*, drifting over the masthead like Cinderella's fairy godmother. What she is actually doing is not completely clear and may be open to various interpretations. She floats in space, that's obvious enough, because there are planets and moons about her; Jupiter clearly identified by its bands. On the left a handsome young couple intently read a copy of the magazine, while on the right an equally well-dressed pair also consult this font—though the latter two are both male. Streams of people seem to be rushing away from the bisexual couple on the left to be strewn, by the giant floating girl, onto the planets in the background. They don't seem to like this because they all come rushing back from the planets on the right to stand behind the two chaps who, understandably, attempt to ignore them. All quite puzzling. Does it mean that SF will take you to the stars which you won't like, then bring you home again to watch two more suckers reading the stuff? Or does the drawing tell us that if a girl and a boy read SF together she will turn into a boy—or be replaced in her co-reader's attention by another lad? Very confusing, and not at all like the contents of the magazine which left very little to the imagination as to what was happening in the stories themselves.

These simple days were soon to end as more and more publishers climbed onto the SF bandwagon. Sensational covers sold magazines. This was their motto, followed by the sub-motto that there was nothing quite as sensational as a girl, preferably in trouble. You didn't have to actually *do* anything to the girls, just the threat would be enough. The adenoidal

readers know very well what will happen in the next instant in time. The groping hand—or tentacle—will clutch more than fabric. Something very frightening, or very satisfying, is about to happen. These two are very often the same thing as the Freudians have been telling us for years, and as science fiction illustration seems to prove.

It does not take a perverted mind to see that all is not sexually kosher in the world of SF art. It is a rare girl that is threatened by anything as obnoxious as a man. A very quick glance will show us girls being threatened by apes, octopi, sea-lion creatures, machines—as well as by a host of alien life that simply defies description. What can they be planning to do with these girls? That is a serious thought that never seems to have occurred to either the art directors or the artists.

These dream creatures certainly cannot be planning to have sexual relationships with the girls. Interspecies sex is rare enough on Earth, practiced only by *homo sapiens*, and is limited to a few domestic animals whose sexual apparatus roughly approximates the human equivalent. To think that aliens from light-year distant planets are dying to have it off with Earth girls is certainly a preposterous assumption. I mean, really, just look at it from the alien's point of view to see how impossible interstellar intercourse appears. Let us travel in our imagination to the fifth planet of the star Alpha Centauri. This is a watery world whose dominant race has a rough exoskeleton very much like that of terrestrial lobsters. One day, on a pleasant beach where the royal princesses are sunning their crunchy green shells, a roaring spaceship lands. From it burst hideous EARTHMEN MONSTERS, soft, damp creatures with wet eyes and fingers like worms. One of them rushes to the prime princess, tears off her girdle of pearls, and . . .

And *what*? All I can think of, attempting to put myself into the boots of a rocketship-riding, lobster-grabbing, interstellar sex fiend is to do—what? I don't get many sexual vibes from the princess. Maybe I can take her pearls back to the rocket and hock them at the nearest comet cathouse. But that is about all.

▶20

"A FOUL ODOR CAME FIRST...THEN, A MASS OF INHUMAN, MONSTROUS CREATURES BEGAN APPEARING AS IF FROM HELL!"
"WITHIN' SECONDS, THEY WERE UPON ME... LUSTFULLY CLUTCHING, PAWING, NUZZLING AT EVERY CONTOUR OF MY PERSON!

What can they be thinking of? When it comes to threat-to-females, science fiction art does not appear to have changed appreciably through the years. Yes, we do see a bit more skin now, some more delicately-rounded female flesh.

But has there been any really basic change? It is still a female being threatened—not a male. It is impossible to find a female, or female-type, monster who is threatening a male human who is garbed only in clinging jockey shorts . . .

Still on the job. Old jokes still the best, old friends still enjoyed, old monsters still after Earth girl, flesh still the standby that sells magazines.

Then why are the alien creatures grabbing the fairest of our womenhood? To eat perhaps? Not good enough. Alien bodies mean alien metabolisms. Can't be done. One alien's flesh is another's poison.

This leaves only two rather remote possibilities; kidnapping and vivisection. Both are minor plot ideas that have appeared from time to time—but not in the numbers needed to explain the sheer quantity of covers of this time. I have never seen a magazine titled either *Stellar Vivisection Stories* or *Interplanetary Kidnapping Tales*.

Having eliminated the hidden we must turn to the glaringly obvious. Girls are on the covers of magazines because girls on covers sell magazines. This is not a theory but a proven publishing principle. Research has been done and surveys made. Certain items sell certain markets. There is the apocryphal story of the survey that proved the three most sales-enhancing items on the *Saturday Evening Post* covers were Abraham Lincoln, doctors and dogs. Which encouraged one writer to submit instantly a story titled *Lincoln's Doctor's Dog*.

Proof of this is in the not-at-all apocryphal story of the *Avon Fantasy Reader*. This was one of the first magazines to attempt to break away from the pulp paper and pulp format to a pocketbook-sized magazine. Donald Wolheim was the editor, a man not only experienced in science fiction but in publishing in general. It contained well-written science fiction and fantasy stories and was a joy to read. It did not sell at all well. The covers on the first issues had strange fantasy creatures doing strange fantasy things, and the sales were so bad the magazine was on the way to going bust. Then the covers changed with the addition of almost-naked girls to the same fantastic scenes. Sales boomed and the magazine was viable.

So that was why girls appeared on pulp SF covers. Ostensibly. But they just weren't girls going about their business in time machines or rockets. They were girls being *threatened*—that is the important point. And threat in this context means sex — whether you like it or not. I am personally no super-Freudian who goes around reading sex into every possible symbol. Freud himself said that there are times when a walking stick is just a walking stick.

No walking sticks here. Girls. Big, lovely, sexy girls. Threat is what is happening to them; no other realistic explanation fits the situation. This is the first subdivision of what our old friend Richard von Krafft-Ebing calls paraesthesia, or perversion of the sexual instinct. Sadism; the associating of sex with lust and cruelty. Basically there are no perversions, or kinky activities, that are not associated with sex. That is what it is all about. While the cleaner-than-clean pulps were keeping good healthy sex out of the front door the sadists, masochists and fetishists were creeping in through the toilet window.

Artists make pictures and pictures can many times be symbols. And the nice thing about symbols is that they don't have to appeal directly to the conscious mind but can instantly strike deeper into the more primitive depths of the subconscious. We have all had the experience of being stirred by a picture, of having an emotional reaction to a pictorial representation without knowing quite *why* we have had the reaction. Esher's unbelievable geometry does something to me that I cannot quite describe, as do Dali's soft watches. I suppose the watches can be logically analyzed as an attempt to describe the plasticity of time, the difference between subjective and objective time that cannot be measured. Now that is all very interesting—but it does not explain the twanging experience I get in my midriff when I look at one of these draped watches. Particularly if it is propped up by a crutch.

Good artists build better than they know. This is true of writers and is certainly true of painters. They pull objects, techniques, visual clues from their subconscious and make them real. Sometimes this is

▶24

Selling copies is always the name of the game. Most copies of most magazines are bought on impulse—and sexual impulse seems to be the charge that sends fingers groping for money. It's obvious which one of these covers sold the most copies.

Can there really be any doubt? The threats come in manifold form, though there are always plenty of heads and teeth. A lot can be read into that, I am sure, and you are welcome to try. But much clearer is who is being threatened. Sexy girl with vanishing clothes. Fine stuff, and straightforward good old sex in the good old days. But things are changing, (opposite). What can the youth of today make of the woman as threat on a cover? Either femlib is triumphing or homosexuality is having its day on display.

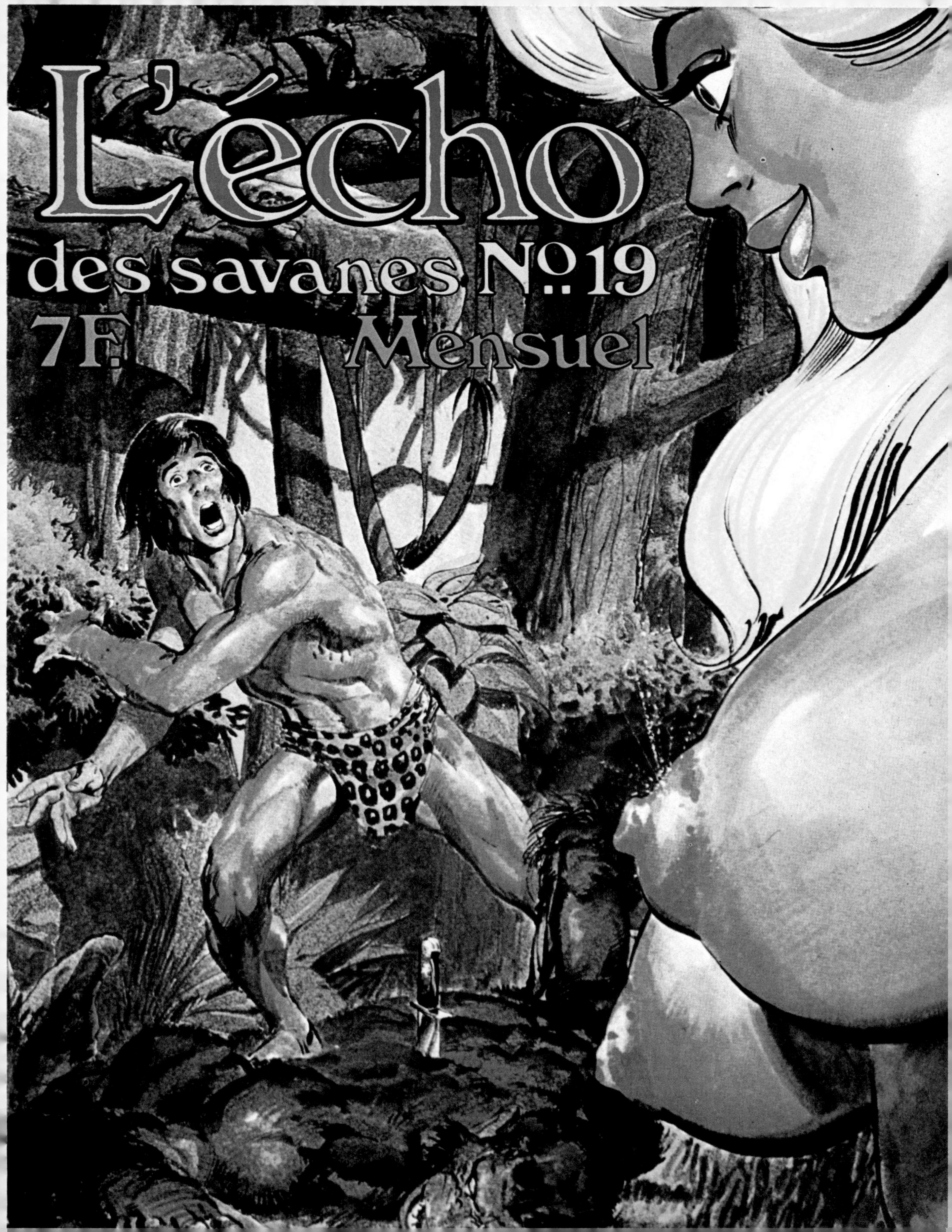
L'écho
des savanes No.19
7F.
Mensuel

deliberate; more often the artist would be hard pressed to explain just what inspired him to get a certain effect. This can certainly be seen in the science fiction artists, many of whom worked for the other pulps as well. All western illustrations are interchangeable, war stories always have soldiers going over the top with explosions, while detectives with guns at the ready have burst open enough doors to keep a battalion of carpenters busy for life. But when these same artists did SF, actually read the story they were to illustrate and made some attempt to capture the atmosphere of the story—why then we had evocative art. The examples are legion and help to explain the popularity of collections of old SF art. They *mean* something, they do something to the viewer, they carry a message.

Many times this message can be painfully clear—to the viewer if not to the artist himself. The first science fiction comics on which a generation of readers was weaned were *Flash Gordon* and *Buck Rogers*. Both were filled with color, action, adventure—and prejudice. That it was the accepted prejudice of the time is no excuse. It was still there. And it was our old friend the Yellow Peril once again.

Buck Rogers falls asleep soon after the First World War in a mine filled with an "unidentified radioactive gas" which makes him sleep for five hundred years. He emerges into a world of rocket pistols, inertron and jumping belts—to help the clean-cut Americans beat off an alien menace. In the words of the author, Philip Nowlan, there were races "whose advance in material civilization had been accompanied by moral and spiritual decay". It comes as no real surprise to discover that they are "... the terrible *Red Mongols*, cruel, greedy and unbelievably ruthless". Buck, of course, helps to polish off these fiends and goes on to conquer the universe.

At the same time other Sunday newspapers were carrying the adventures of Flash Gordon, one of the most beautifully drawn comics to ever appear. In this strip a rogue planet approaches Earth on a collision course. Disaster is prevented by a mad scientist named Dr. Zarkov who crashes into it with a home-built

(This page above) The first picture, Prince Barin in his original and bald existence. The second shows the not-too-subtle change of Barin from baddy to goody—complete with skin bleach and hairpiece. And this is what the well dressed girl of the future wore in the 1930's. (Opposite below) Buck Rogers guarding the honour of sexy Wilma Deering.

rocketship manned by two kidnapped companions. The crash forces the planet, Mongo, out of orbit so it misses the Earth. Then Zarkov, Flash and Dale emerge from the wreck! So much for Alex Raymond's scientific knowledge—but he could still draw like a dream. Our travellers are captured by soldiers and brought before the emperor, Ming the Merciless. In case readers should be in doubt as to Ming's antecedants he has bright yellow skin and the same drooping moustachios as the Red Mongols. If racial intolerance were not so distasteful this sort of thing would be ludicrous. The author-artist—or his subconscious—will not even allow good guys to have the wrong color skin. In the early sequences Prince Barin was one of the enemy, complete with bald dome, slant eyes and yellow hide. Later, as the plot twisted, he joined Flash and became a goody. At which point the yellow drained from his skin and turned into a nice Miami tan, the ends of his moustache perked up—and he grew a college crewcut. So much for symbols!

Despite these faults, *Flash Gordon* will always be treasured for its luscious girls. They were always losing their clothes—or having them torn away—and the revealing and sexy outfits they wore inspired a generation of artists. Raymond's art shaped the future of futuristic costume design in all the other media.

Science fiction artists were always dead serious. But they must surely have had very active subconscious minds. Here is a cover (opposite left) that contains enough symbolism—woman riding man, woman with gun, chains, man immobilized for a doctoral thesis.

3

Strange Relations

It really is very hard to keep all those aliens at bay. Defying all logic they still cannot keep their hands (paws, claws, tentacles, hooks, suckers) off our human girls. Not satisfied with simply threatening these nubile creatures, as we have seen, they now procede to *carry them away*.

What a way to go—and away they went! Paws, claws, tentacles, fingers . . . they just can't get enough of our luscious Earth girls. And it's still going on, the only change today being (opposite, below) that the girls have a lot more flesh showing.

Girl-carrying could almost be called a sub-category of science fiction art. The examples are numerous and fascinating. Firstly—look who is doing the carrying. With a quick glance I see girls, raiment suitably torn, being carried off by a King Kong sized ape, a fish man, a bird man, a blue man, a clawed space ship and a giant bicycle wheel. Where can they be going? What can these creatures be planning? If there is any doubt about what is going to happen to these helpless creatures we have but to look at the expressions on the face of the occasional man who carries off a girl. Is that a wicked leer or is that not a wicked leer? Our earlier guess about sex off-cover seems to be proven. Sex, once again, is the name of the game.

A firm bit of evidence in this direction would be the rescue-by-flying illustrations. This is a theme that is pictured again and again. Here a man swoops down on a space sled, a porto-flyer, a pair of wings—or is just being towed along by a ball of force. (Must I mention what the ball symbolizes?) Whisk and up, up and away. It might be useful to recognize that, when this aerial rescue appears, both male and female share the same expression, one much more peaceful and tranquil than the forceful-removal ones. In Freudian terms flying is synonymous with intercourse; even the staunchest non-Freudian, after one look at this art, would have to agree with that.

Hint, hint, hint—is that all we are to get? Yes, for the best part of thirty years. Even when the stories started to mature the art did not. The clichés were fixed and unchangeable. The pattern set and hard, almost impossible to alter. As the old artists faded from sight the new ones came on stage and picked up the stock symbols and situations. It is interesting to note just how consistent over the years these props were.

Look at the obvious sexual dimorphism for instance. Now the one thing about mankind, which includes womankind, is the fact that sexual dimorphism is not terribly marked. This means that both sexes look very much alike. Now, before you sneer and point at *that*, not to mention *that*, I hurry to agree that there are

▶32

THE NEW LIFE
JOHN COLERIDGE
MEN WITHOUT
A WORLD
MARCH
15c

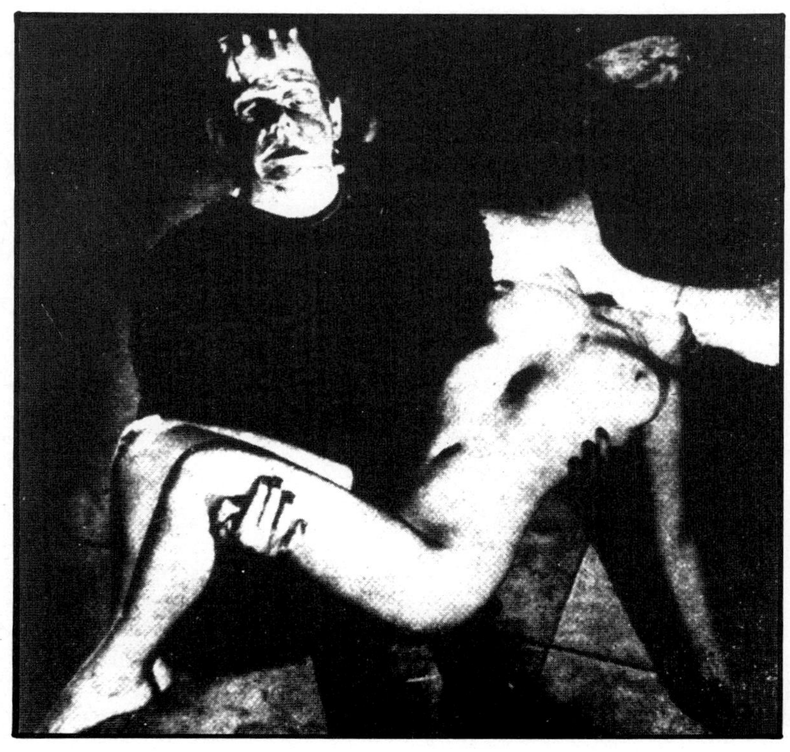

Screaming was very much in order—for good reason!—when the uglies grabbed the girls. Blissful expectation or satiation (opposite, and above) was reserved for roughly-human males. And the carrying goes on to this day. One of the rare exceptions (above right) from well before the days of femlib, actually has the girl doing the job.

differences, but they are not outstandingly obvious. In the good old days we had no problem in telling the guys from the dolls. But this was mostly a matter of artificially enhanced features and constructed differences. Clothes are an example of artificial distinctions. Girls were not born in high heels, short skirts and silk stockings. They also used to curl their hair and paint their faces in interesting patterns. Then came unisex and the differences were no longer obvious. With long hair, no make-up, loose sweaters and blue jeans, one has to stare closely to determine the sex of the subject. Many times even this does not work and, short of a quick grope in the right area, there is no easy way now to tell.

Sexual dimorphism is not, therefore, as marked in *homo sapiens* as it is in other animals. When we see a lion's mane we know that he is the he, not the sleek and maneless female. When the female elephant seal snuggles up to her mate we know who is who—undoubtedly since he is twenty times bigger than she. Look at the birds, the prancing peacock and the drab peahen, and all the ducks, and you can tell instantly whose job it is to lay the eggs. Look, with a bit of awe, at some of the lesser animals such as the marine worm where the male of one species has degenerated to a small brain, a bit of spinal column—attached to a tremendous sex organ of much greater size than the pendant parts. This degenerate chap, if he can be called that, lives permanently in the vagina of the female which explains why he has no need for a brain at all. (Just keep all the obvious analogies to yourself.)

But while sexual dimorphism is not marked in terrestrial mankind, it is certainly more than obvious in the members of our species who venture into space and go to the far planets. Just look at the men. They are usually garbed in something that looks like rubberized sailcloth, occasionally skintight, but more often bumpy and baggy. They wear thick gloves and heavy boots and seem to always have a gun of some kind in one hand. Only their heads are visible through the fishtank apparatus they wear; a lucky choice or they would not be able to see at all.

Now let us look at the female. She will also wear a fishtank over her head, since breathing is a necessity—but here the resemblance changes markedly. Instead of heavy fabric she is wrapped in transparent plastic like a candy box. (The comparison is not accidental.) Under the plastic she wears very little, or *very little* as we say in science fiction, the italicized word being one of the few writing tools available that indicates stress for a number of writers. Skintight briefs, the mons Veneris well outlined, kinky boots, and either a bikini top . . .

Or brass breastplates.

These bits of body armour seem to be exclusive to science fiction, a good deal of searching has failed to uncover them in any other place. Yet they are quite prevalent in SF art. All of the legions of space Amazons wear them. This is a completely modern myth because

➧36

Although the clichés remain the same, the freedom of the artist has advanced through the years. A typical pulp illustration (opposite, top) suggests, while the modern (above) reveals all.

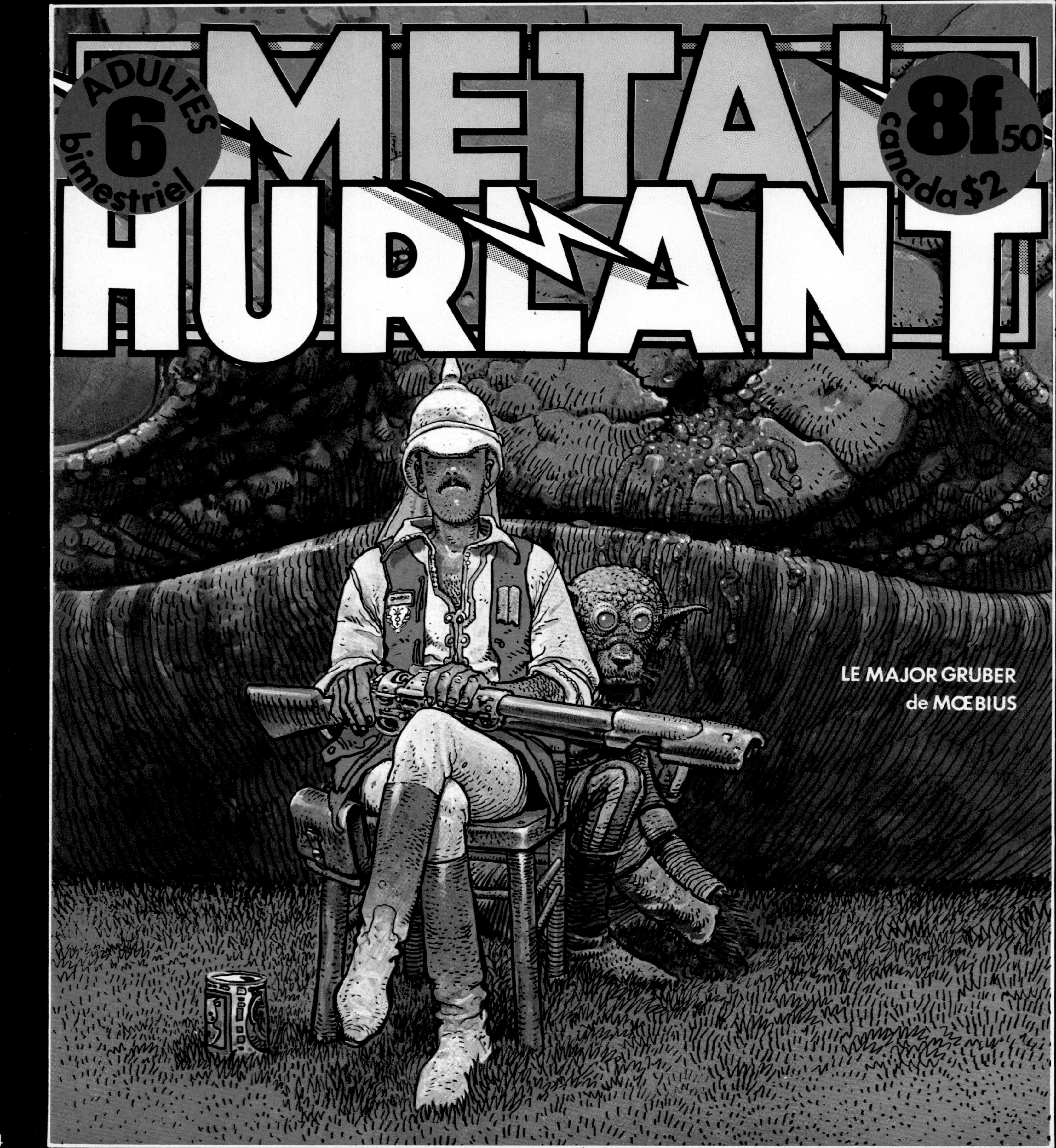
METAL HURLANT
ADULTES
6
bimestriel
8f50
canada $2
LE MAJOR GRUBER
de MŒBIUS

METAL HURLANT
RESERVE AUX ADULTES!
no. 10
8,50f.
canada $2

As advanced, and talented, as the modern French artists are, they are not going to abandon the noble tradition of sexual dimorphism. Even hunters of alien beasts (previous pages) have to dress correctly for the part. The artist Earl Bergey (this page, right) brought the art of the brass bra to its highest polish. Only today (opposite, below) do we see what we have been missing down through the years. (Overpage) There is the ultimate in chic brass bizarrerie.

the Amazons of history and legend went bare-breasted. In fact they were purported to have cut off one breast so it would not get twanged by the bow string when they fired off their arrows. Bare breasts have always had connotations with women's strength. In the Norse Saga of Thorfinn Karlsefni his wife, Gudrid, sends the Vinland natives, the *skraelling,* into a flight of panic when she bares her breasts to them and slaps them with her sword.

So why the SF brass breastplates? Once again we must turn to the glaringly obvious. Like lipstick to draw the eye to the full and sensuously wet lips, like a deep cleavage to attract attention to the bosom, the gleaming breastplates draw attention to what is concealed within. Also, as with the traditional sequined black-lace panties, they conceal and enhance at the same time.

The only subtlety in all of this, if it can be called that, is the placing of the action in space or on an alien planet. This removes the scene from current events and customs. (Remember the bare breasts on the black girls in the jungle?) Unhampered by modern garb our artist is free to indulge himself in whatever wickedness his subconscious, or the art director, dictates. Firstly, get rid of the hero. Boys read SF, not girls, and they want to look at the female form. So on with the rubberized spacesuit and into the background with the male. But don't forget to put a gun in his hand; when you have a potent phallic symbol make the most of it. Now to the girl! Lips full and sensual, hair long and luscious. Built like a tank and all the curves revealed. Breastplates for reasons already given, boots for reasons to come. Then decorate the whole thing with monsters, ships, balls of fire, lightning, everything. Not a bad day's work. Into the editor with the art and down to the bar with the check for a reviving drink. The end of happy day in the simple life of an SF illustrator.

PLANET
STORIES
OF VENUS
CAVE-DWELLERS
OF SATURN

STARTLING
STORIES
15¢
A THRILLING PUBLICATION
THE DAY OF THE BEAST
Shadow OVER MARS
An Amazing Complete Novel
By LEIGH BRACKETT

STARTLING
STORIES
A THRILLING PUBLICATION
FEATURING
TETRAHEDRA OF SPACE
A Hall of Fame Classic

ICI, JE SUIS DIFFÉRENTE!

4

A Matter of Plumbing

One of the never-solved riddles of SF art is just why the robots and machine men should show such a burning interest in female Earthlings. Aliens are a different matter. Being made of flesh and blood, or something squishy very much like flesh and blood, their interests can partially be understood. Or if not their interests, then the hidden drive of artist and art director that enables these creatures to stand in for human males or even for the darkest desires of the human reader.

This cannot be true of the robots. That they have an overwhelming desire to do something to the girls is obvious since they are so often in hot pursuit, and seen equally often carrying off their screaming victims.

It just *can't* be sex. If robots do it with each other it can't be very interesting, more like attaching a hosepipe to a tap than any decent form of orgasmic intercourse. While we can imagine a perverted plumber fixing up a robot for copulation, it is hard to imagine the robot getting any fun out of it. Sex without pleasure and orgasm isn't very much like sex at all.

Therefore, as the robot is not really up to anything personal, he must be the stand-in for someone else. If he is operating under instructions in the story or the art—the mad professor in the background pointing the way is pretty clear—then all is understandable. The robot is just the tool being used for a human's nefarious ends.

But what if he is obviously alone? If he is a machine man on a machine world—what then? Vivisection and kidnapping again, but that can't be the complete explanation.

Of course it isn't. The robot is a stand-in for the reader, the libidinous young man who is getting his jollies from his favorite form of fiction. This is probably not the reason he went to this literature in the first place, since there have always been plenty of specialist magazines that cater to this eternal need. No, this is a fringe benefit, something unexpected yet appreciated all the same. Appreciated mostly because it is not overt. The few magazines that attempted to publish slightly-sexy SF in the early days folded rather quickly. The fans

Every boy's symbol of power—the indestructible robot, able, even, to crunch the superheroes. Very serious stuff. Except to the French (opposite) who add a touch of Gallic wit—and some even more interesting interpretation when we think of what rockets are symbols for . . .

and readers did not like it. They wanted their favorite fiction pure—at least on the surface. This was supposed to be a literature of the brain not the groin, something better than the others. Born of the pulps yet not a pulp.

The robot is a modern science fiction invention and should be recognized as such. He may take his name from Čapek's play, R.U.R., but it should be remembered that Rossum's Universal Robots would not be called robots today but androids. They are descendants of Mary Shelley's Frankenstein monster, who can trace his lineage back through the Golem and beyond; creatures who look human yet who were made, not born. They are human in all except navel and birth trauma and legions of them have marched through science fiction. But they are not robots.

Robots are supermen, with all of mankind's strengths and none of his failings. They are better designed to begin with. And look at their attributes. Stronger, faster, sleeker, brighter, longer-lived, more functional, capable of infinite repair—incapable of death. They can often rise to loyalty and love and all of the other human emotions. They can do anything a human being can do and do it better. Except one thing. Sex.

If early pulp SF was boy's fiction, then the robot is every boy's ideal of himself as a figure of power. The strongest, biggest, best guy on the block. And the one who doesn't have to worry about going blind, getting warts on the palms of his hands—or about being involved with the worry, the pressures, the desires, the continual disturbances of the onslaught of puberty. Oh happy robot, would that I could but be you! Just hit that mighty muscle with a hammer and hear the metallic clang! Not a problem in the world that cannot be solved by muscle or brain, both of which he has to perfection.

Mensuel pour adultes!
NO.9
8,50f.
canada $2
Bandes Dessinées
d'Humour et de
Science-Fiction
TARDI

Yes, but, if all this is true—why are you carrying off the girl?

Who says that we have to stick to one symbol, image or drive? Certainly not the psychiatrists who see all problems shading off into other problems. As a robot it doesn't mean we don't want to carry off a nubile wench or two when we get the chance; our dreams don't exist only in the robot mode. The heterosexual drives are still applying the lash. Our robot persona can carry the girl off so our hero persona can have a good go at her. What's wrong with that?

Nothing at all—as long as we keep it perfectly clear as to who is doing what, with which, and to whom. Daydreams come in all plots and colors. And there is no rule that says that all desires and fears have to be sexual. Some people do insist that all of our problems are basically sexual but this is simplistic to say the least. There are other crisis situations and external pressures in the world as well. If a man is depressed because he is out of a job, sick and starving I really feel that sex is not his problem. Social pressures do affect literature, and one of the most prevalent in modern fiction has been xenophobia. Two astute critics, Leslie Fiedler and Brian W. Aldiss, both point out that the hordes of great apes, clanking monstrosities and lascivious aliens are no more than stand-ins for the Red Indian and the Black Man. Referring to pulp magazine covers where a white girl is tied naked to a stake while savage redskins dance and howl about her, Fiedler writes, "... it panders to the basic white male desire at once to relish and deplore, vicariously share and publicly condemn, the rape of White female innocence." That there may be a good deal of truth in this theory can be proven by a simple glance at the SF covers of the Girls Threatened and the Girls Being Carried Off categories. While the threateners and carriers come in all sizes, shapes, colors and degrees of loathsomeness, the girls have one factor in common.

All of them are healthily pink, fine examples of the White Race. Not a Black, Yellow, Red or colored girl among them.

In science fiction there are many pressures and drives other than sex. If we wish to put aside, if ever so briefly, all of the problems involving women, we can turn to what has been called the very best SF magazine of them all, which for many years *was* the very best magazine of them all, the magazine of the mind not the glands, which never had any truck with female flesh. *Astounding*, that was the name. ▶46

Inside that invincible robot there is a small boy lurking—or a frustrated young man. (This page) Science fiction had an all male readership when this cover was done. In Freudian terms flying means sexual intercourse so (opposite) there is little doubt as to what is happening here.

RMB

THE LITTLE SPACE PIONEER

PAR MOEBIUS

THANK GOD I'VE GOT THIS CUTE ROBOT TO KEEP ME WARM IN MY ANTI-G BUNK

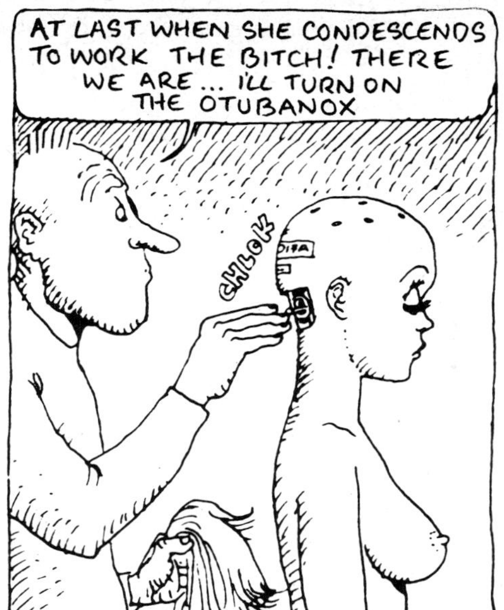
AT LAST WHEN SHE CONDESCENDS TO WORK THE BITCH! THERE WE ARE... I'LL TURN ON THE OTUBANOX
CHLOCK

GOOD! NOW THEN I'LL TURN IT TO "GREAT TENDERNESS"
CLIC

DARLING, I'M HERE
ZZGBL

SON OF A ROTTEN PHALLOCRATIC BASTARD! I'LL MAKE YOU EAT YOUR BALLS

COME BACK HERE YOU BUGGER!
SUFFERING SPACE! THE BREAKDOWN DIDN'T COME FROM THE SPITROPIT!
PILOT

WOE! EVERYTHING HAS TO BE DONE AGAIN... MASTURBATION WILL CONTINUE TO PREVAIL IN THIS SHIP!
FIN

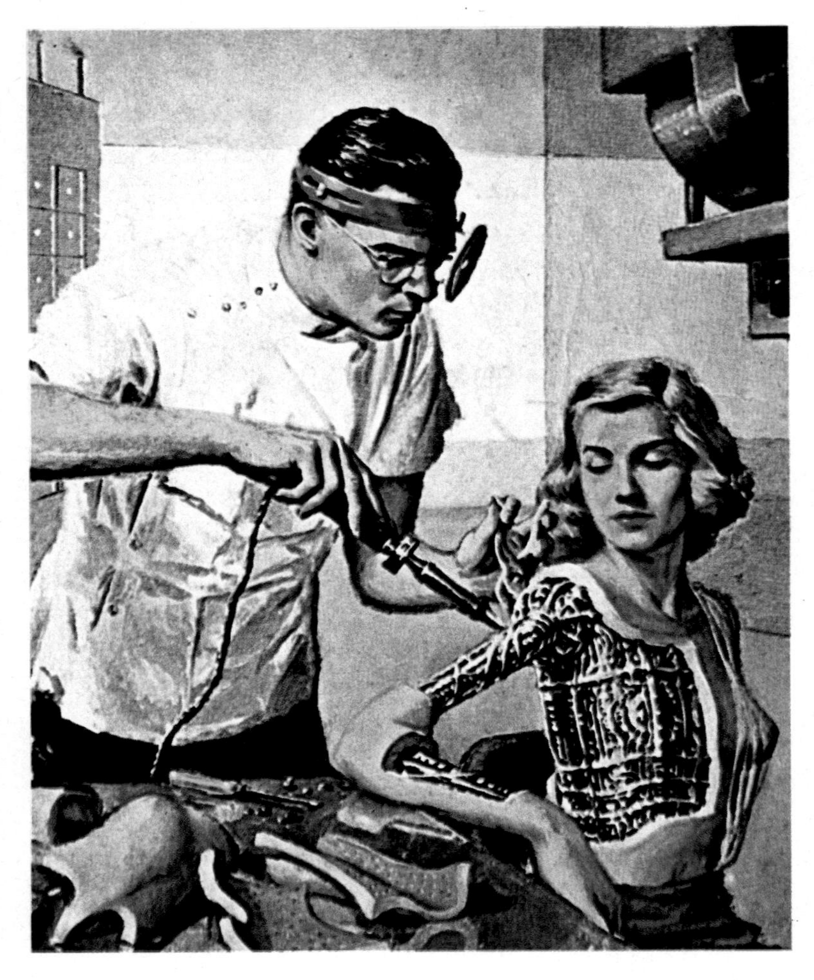

Robots, like golem, are built to physically symbolize desires and beliefs. What then do we make of the female robot? The easy answer is that it is a motorized sex machine (this page). The doctor's outfit is a fake. He is building a woman that he can control, at last, in every way; an American dream, that gains new significance once it crosses the Atlantic to France, (previous pages). Once again juvenile libidinous dreams—but with an unexpected outcome.

John W. Campbell invented modern science fiction; no one will deny that. He reached in and grabbed it by the neck, hauled it out of the mud wallow of the pulps and washed it clean under the cold shower of reason. Logic had everything to do with it. Here was the entire galaxy opened before us, ready to be explored. He was not a theoretical literary aggrandizer, he just *knew* that science fiction was the best game in town. When asked if he thought that mainstream would some day take over science fiction—or vice versa—he would dramatically explain just what regions SF covered. He would hold his left hand up and say that here is the birth of the universe, the big bang. He would then throw his arms wide and wiggle his right hand, saying that was the other extreme, the end, the heat death of the universe. In between was everything, all time and matter and life, the legitimate stamping ground of science fiction. Then, holding two fingers closely together he would put them in the middle of the space he had just delineated.

"Here," he would say deeply and slowly, "here, between my fingers is all of the other literature of mankind. A very small part of that is mainstream fiction."

Not only did John Campbell mean this, but he acted as if it were true. For all the long decades that he edited *Astounding Science Fiction*, later to be retitled *Analog Science Fact-Science Fiction*, he lived up to this vision—and saw to it that his writers and readers did as well. With all of the universe to deal with and straighten out, sex got pinched away between those same fingers along with mainstream fiction. There were just more important things to do. One does not expect to find saucy stories in a calculus text and, for exactly the same reasons, one did not expect to find it in the pages of ASF. John Campbell was not against sex and human emotions; away from his magazine he was a passionate and kindly man, a paterfamilias, warm to his friends, a figure of wrath to his enemies. His authors, though, were—and are—definitely interested in sex in every way.

There was the occasional story in ASF that at least nodded its head in the direction of love and sexuality, but these were usually as soppy and maudlin as a drunken electronic engineer—and just as entertaining; perhaps put there as a warning of what not to do. In the longer serials, eventually published as novels, intersexual relationships did have their place,

though always in a hearty familial way, and offstage to boot. Kimball Kinnison, the mighty Lensman, went through serial after serial and eventually begot a dynasty of little lensmen out of the fair body of Clarissa MacDougal. (It was an Anglo-Saxon and Celtic galaxy.) But the children were conceived and born between volumes of the saga, and fully grown before they appeared in the pages of the magazine. Though nothing sexual was intended, as a reading of the surrounding copy quickly reveals, the Lensman series was the setting for the only undraped form ever to grace the pages of ASF. Nothing very shocking, but worth recording for its rarity like the one-cent black British Guiana postage stamp.

Science fiction category magazines were born in the twenties and flourished in the thirties. Like all of publishing they staggered through the war years of the forties and only began to change in any appreciable manner in the fifties. Until this miniboom in magazine SF, which was shared by the book publishers, nothing had really changed since the Campbell revolution.

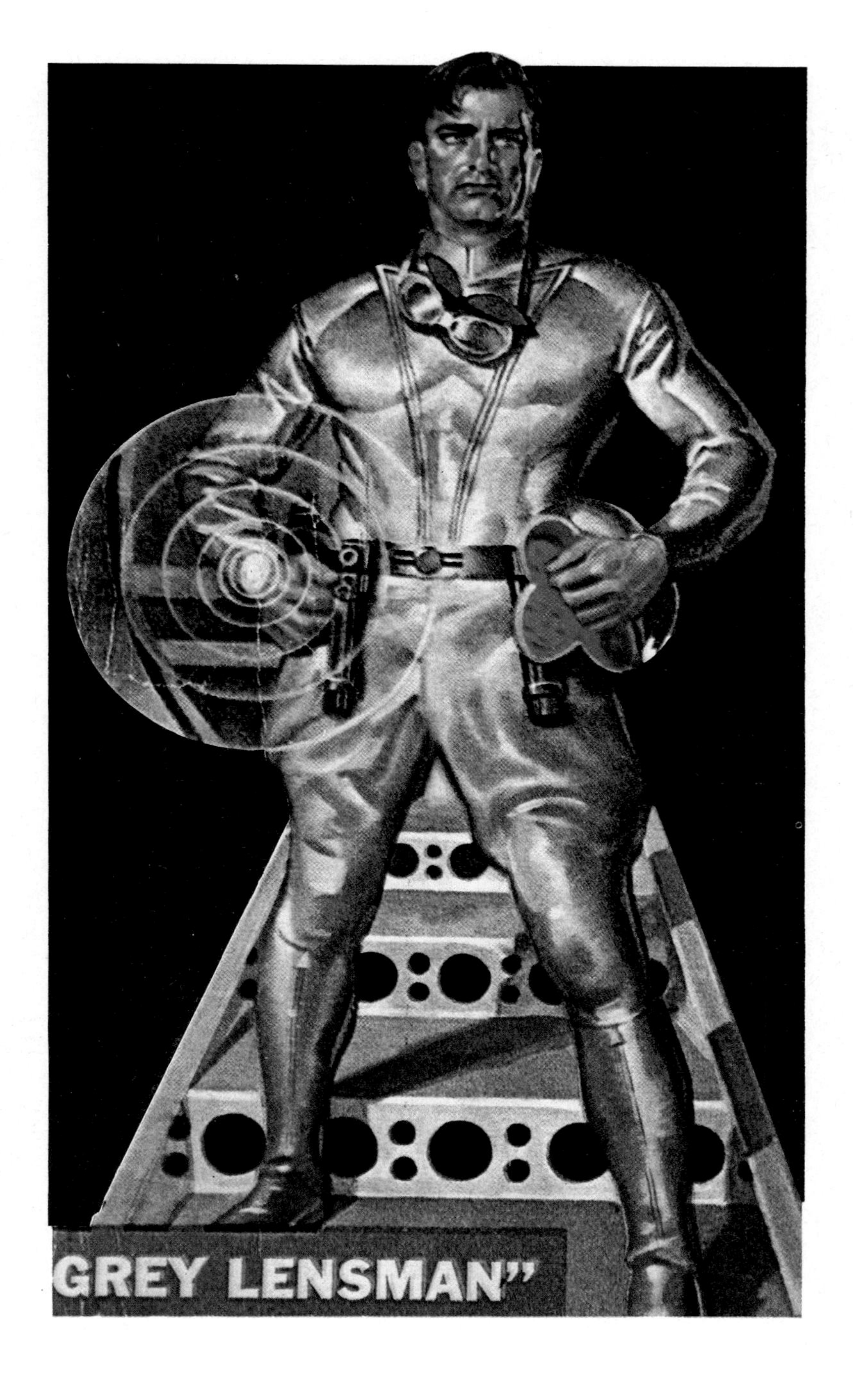

Kimball Kinnison, the Lensman, every boy's power symbol—and a young boy himself in every way. No sex, no girls—but plenty of old chums, alien and human, to aid him in destroying the enemy, always in the goriest way possible.

Great art (this page) but unreadable contents. The Palmer magazines, 'Amazing' and 'Fantastic', contained only stories aimed at a juvenile market, and written to order by hacks. Only the artwork had any quality—to induce the boyish buyer to part with his small change. It wasn't until the 70's that this changed when Les Humanoids Associes matched quality art to strong story (opposite page).

Astounding embodied one certain kind of science fiction and made no compromises. The covers showed machines, robots, rockets, gadgets, anything at all that might illustrate the contents of the magazine, with no attempt ever to get female flesh in just for the fun of it. (Or for the fun of the sales figures.) Then there was the rest of the world. The other magazines ran the gambit all the way from good to trash. They all looked alike and generally read alike, although the occasional excellent editor like Samuel Mines would sneak excellent stories, and occasionally revolutionary stories, into a magazine that resembled all the others. Physically they were hard to tell apart. The best illustrations were reserved for the Ray Palmer *Amazing* and *Fantastic*, where the finest artists illustrated the worst crud. Perhaps to prove the consistent inconsistancy of science fiction, there were the Lowndes magazines which always paid the bottom rate but got some of the best stories. Yet the art budget there was so low that the terrible drawings enjoyed a zombie-like existence. After first appearing as full page spreads, they were sawn into quarters and the resulting blocks used to illustrate four other stories in later issues of the magazines.

But in all of the magazines the sex was in the illustrations, not in the stories. More was suggested than was revealed; plenty of hints but few outright statements.

One of the strongest hints was that there is more to sex than just boy meets girl.

PSYCHOROCK

METAL HURLANT

Bimestriel
Pour Adultes

NO. 8

10 F

Canada $2

SPECIAL ETE
100 PAGES

5
The Whip Cracks—or is Krafft-Ebing?

Is there any form of fiction that is completely free of sex? I doubt it very much, because sex appears in interesting disguises in the oddest of places. Science fiction illustrations provide a tropical jungle of the strangest and most exotic growths.

Variations on the sexual theme are as diverse as mankind's range of cultures. The Victorians were horrified at these alternate possibilities and considered them heathen, something practiced by the most perverted of native tribes. They themselves, though, were probably the most twisted of tribes since repression led Victorian gentlemen into some of the most exotic perversions ever recorded. It was a pillar of European Victorian Age society himself who recorded the interesting goings-on of the middle classes, Richard, Baron von Krafft-Ebing. A German, as his name might have suggested, he recorded his labor in that still fascinating volume, *Psychopathia Sexualis.*

Although Krafft-Ebing made every attempt to be abstract in his observations, he was still rather biased with his value judgments. While maintaining a cool and abstract attitude towards his fellow burghers and their continuing interest in coprophilia, he condemned cunnilingus and fellatio as disgusting practices of the rougher sections of the working classes. Win one, lose one. What he did do, that is so important, was to record case history after case history, to study sex rather than ignore it, to open the door to legitimate investigation so that the Johnsons and Masters of the later era could accomplish their important tasks.

Krafft-Ebing studied what he called paraesthesia, or perversion of the sexual instinct. We live in a more understanding age now and these practices are referred to as—paraphilia, aberrant sexual activity. The three major divisions he was concerned with are still with us: sadism, masochism, and fetishism.

Sadism is the association of lust and cruelty with sex, and science fiction illustration proves a happy hunting ground for examples of art of this kind. It does as well for sadism's counterpart, masochism, where suffering is a source of sexual pleasure.

Sadism, substituting violence for sexual aggression, is subtly shown in much SF art—or very unsubtly indeed (left). It was always the girls who were tortured, of course. Women then were passive, frightened little things. Today's girl has no such inhibitions, (opposite) she's more than a match for the men. Now, the boot is really on the other foot, and magazine publishers are no longer afraid of showing the violence that previously had only been hinted at.

In many ways the SF art is far more interesting than all the books and magazines sold at the sex shops around the world. Everything is overt in these publications, and far too clinical. The mystery is gone, as well as the indirection, which is the heart of the matter in the first place. All those whips, chains and high black boots are ways of directing attention away from, or of substituting one thing for the important other. Since science fiction is the literature of dreaming—why not a little sexual dreaming as well?

Why not indeed! All at once new meaning is breathed into many an SF cover. Wish fulfillment, the carrying off of the bound and struggling virgin is certainly not a new idea in art. From the Rape of the Sabines on there has been no shortage of art with this particular message. The pulps and particularly the SF pulps carried this to a fine art. (Nor was it that hard for the artists to switch from category to category. Rescue by dragon or rescue by horse is really the same thing as we can see on the next page.) How often the tentacles and claws that carry off the damsel also tighten a *little* too hard so we also get a quick burst of sadism across the bows.

Once more, if there was any doubt that this was all happening by chance, it is obvious that it is the girls that are getting into trouble. The men occasionally get tied up, but they quickly escape, and if captured all they do while bound is stand there and glare. The girls respond more interestingly with plenty of writhing, screaming and clothes-tearing. This is sex and no two ways about it.

For the Freudians science fiction is a rich pasture

Riding to the rescue—with implied seduction to follow—was a pulp standby. There wasn't too much of this in the stories, but the covers specialized in it. (Opposite, left) Change the horse for a monster and you had SF instead of a western.

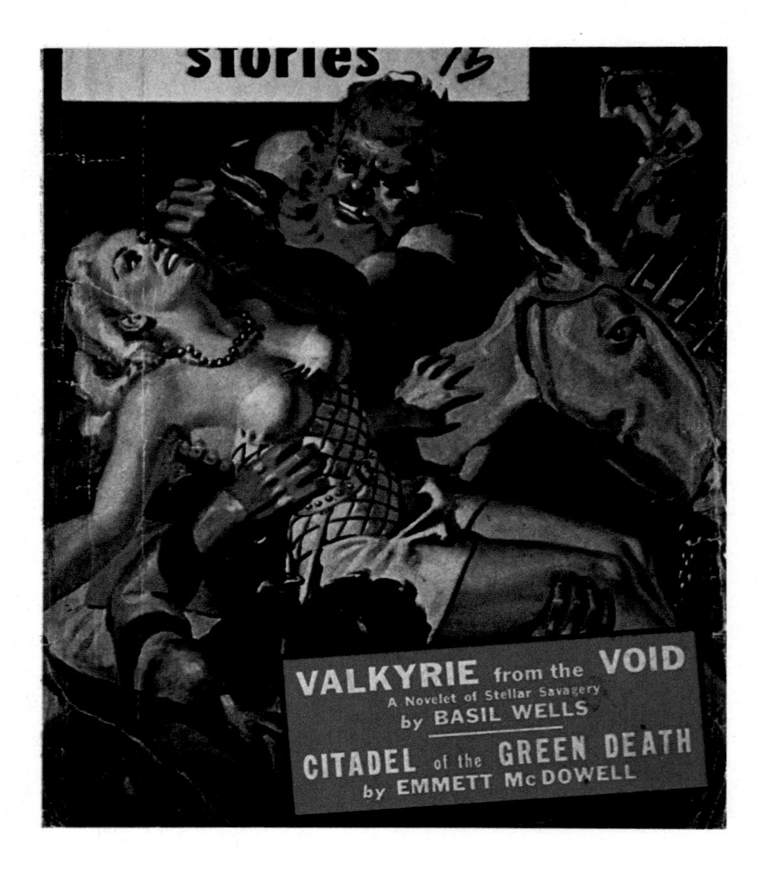

indeed. If one believes that perversions are fragments of inhibited development at an early stage, infantilism in fact, why there are examples galore. If thumb sucking is an example of oral eroticism—then what about all those spacesuits with the water and food teats inside that the hero can suck away at to his heart's content? In fact there is perversion inside a reversion since the spacesuit itself is obviously a return to the womb. How Freud would have loved science fiction! What could he not have done with these wombsuit-spacesuits which not only supplied all needs but took away all waste with the orifices plugged into tubes and pipes?

The overt and covert sexual nature of many illustrations is more obvious in the comic books. They reached their zenith of success during and after the war. The men in the services loved them and they could do double service as reading matter in the latrine, where the most specific form of literary criticism could be exercised. Unlike the pulp magazines, the comics could be published with little or no restraints on their contents. By comparison even the smallest pulp publisher could afford at least a part-time art director, and there was always at least one editor and, always, the publisher, to actually look at what was being printed. While some of the larger comic book publishers did look like real publishers, with offices, secretaries, editors and all of that apparatus, a good number of them published in thin air.

Lest I be accused of manufacturing this wild story out of wold cloth I must present my *bona fides*. I am a writer and it is common knowledge that no one is ever trained to be a writer. Jacket copy on books always mentions the early and exotic occupations of authors: lumberjacks, loggers, private detectives, pig farmers, stevedores and such like. While I wish I had done a stint as a pig farmer, I think they are fine beasts, I am forced to admit that my earlier labors were much closer to home. Home being publishing. Trained as a fine artist, I ended up as a commercial artist. In comics. I drew the things, wrote the things, lettered in the balloons, edited them and even published them. I went from comics into pulps, editing, writing and illustrating them as well. So when I speak about comics I speak from a position, as it were,somewhere back among the molars in the horse's mouth.

Many comic publishers were just black paint on an office door. If you had a distributor's contract you were a publisher; it was as simple as that. For a few grand you too could bring excitement into the lives of

thousands. With the contract you got an engraver and a printer, because the distributor guaranteed to pay both these bills when the magazines were delivered. The least important thing was producing the magazine itself. This particular function was farmed out.

Here is how it worked. The "publisher" would use his lawyer's address as a company address. The name of the new company, Sado-Maso Love Stories, Inc., would be painted on the lawyer's door. At a prearranged time the publisher would leave expensive suburbia to meet the editor-packager—who shaved and dressed as well as he could in his slum apartment—at the lawyer's office. A new magazine was about to be born; the editor would dry-wash his hand in anticipation. It would be called *Horror Romances*. The editor's fee would be $100 an issue, and an equally cheeseparing budget for contents would be announced, a deadline declared. Agreed? Agreed. Out into the chill streets of New York City and to the telephone and another new magazine would be on its way.

For his fee the editor would contact other starving artists and writers who would work for the lowest fees. The scripts for the stories would be written, the stories drawn, a cover drawn as well to imitate the best selling comics in the field—as would the new title. The complete comic would then be delivered to the publisher who, after alternately being threatened and cajoled, would reluctantly pay up on the bills presented for the work. In order to make both ends meet the editor would probably write and draw most of the magazine himself, then submit bills under a number of different names. ("This Lee Da Vinci is a great artist, and the new writer Charley Dickens is good too.")

▶58

SF art can be a garden of nightmares. Hannes Bok was the gentlest of men but (left) his female kneecaps would certainly make any prospective lover uncomfortable. It is rare indeed that all indirection is discarded (below) and we get the true quill, sadistic sexual torture at its nubile best. But modern heroines are no longer weak little women; they fight back (opposite), appropriately well-built and unencumbered by clothing.

GET AWAY FROM ME OR I'LL **HARM** YOU.

Occasionally the publisher would have things redrawn and pushed around just to prove he was the publisher, but most of the time the magazine went directly to the engraver—after a careful count to see if there were the right number of pages.

Who was responsible for the contents? No one—if responsibility means care, attention and physical presence in case of lawsuits, protests or feedback of any kind. By the time the thing was published and ready for the hordes of drooling infants lined up with their dimes ready, the "publishing firm" would have vanished like a puff of yesterday's cigarette smoke. The publisher would have another front corporation painted on the lawyer's door, the editor would be in pauper's prison or would have re-enlisted in the Army to get a square meal, the artists dead of an overdose or earning an honest living in carwashes. So who cared what went into the comics? The answer is that no one did, really. Sincere artists and dedicated editors could turn out works of art that sold six copies because they had lousy distribution, while inflamed examples of moronic violence sold in the hundreds of thousands when they caught the readers' fancy—and the right distribution.

So it is that in the comics we find sex delineated more clearly than in the pulps. That crusading campaigner of comic cleanliness, Dr. Frederick Wertham, spelled it out as clearly as this in the *Seduction of the Innocent*.

"Comic books stimulate children sexually", the good doctor wrote. "One of the stock mental aphrodisiacs in comic books is to draw breasts in such a way that they are sexually exciting. Whenever possible they protrude and obtrude, or girls are shown in slacks or negligees with their pubic regions indicated with special care and suggestiveness."

Very true. Not all of the time, not even most of the time. But often enough. At the height of the comic boom in the fifties there were over 600 different titles being published a month. When you consider that the minimum print run then for a comic was 200,000 copies, a wave of multicoloured crud in excess of 120,000,000 copies was washing over the news-

Dark things do tend to clutch girls on these magazine covers. (This page and opposite) Unlike the robot clutches, the objects they wave at the girls, spikes and tentacles, are obvious phallic symbols. But I still insist that these are the fruits of the artist's subconscious. Look at this SF horror comic (right) with its groping hands and torn dress. Symbolism? No, instructions. The publisher thought a lot of hands doing this would be kind of fun and told the artist so. The clod simply did what he had been ordered to do with no thought of poisoning minds or being devious. I know. I was the artist.

How Dr Wertham, that chronicler of comic book sins, would have loved this! It has everything—including a whiff of subtlety with those tentacles.

stands of the nation every four weeks. Entire forests sacrificed! Most of this was kiddy stuff with little talking animals, or saccharine romances, boring westerns, costumed heroes and detectives and the like. Then there was the crap. Produced in the carefully discerning manner I have just outlined.

Like so much bad in this world it was not done out of malice and perversion. Just stupidity. I remember one publisher for whom I packaged a science fiction title, a romance and a horror magazine. (Yes, I imagine you have already recognized the shambling editor, so thinly disguised.) Horror magazines were something new then, and had not risen to the heights—nor sunk to the depths—they later reached. They featured simple stories of corpses returning from the sea for revenge, or disembodied hands seeking revenge, or ghosts keening for revenge. They were far more boring than horrible. I would meet the publisher once a month, in the lawyer's office of course, and turn in the bundle of illustration boards that made up a magazine. I knew that he believed that horror consisted of bones, skulls and skeletons and little else. So no matter how much the cover I presented resembled a disinterred ossuary it was never enough. Therefore I came equipped with more bones and skulls cut out of paper, as well as a jar of rubber cement. He would chortle to himself and point out the right spots and I would glue bones on all over the new cover like a mad osteologist. Occasionally even this would not be enough and he would pick the extra bones off the previous issue's cover and I would glue these on as well. It didn't matter that half of these showered off on the way to the engraver, leaving a trail of leprechaun skeletons down the corridor. The publisher was happy! He never bothered to look at the stories inside the book. But he was satisfied. For example, I worked for another publisher whose editor was so crooked that I had to pay *him* five dollars a page kickback before he would accept the work. Then he would count the pages from the edges—without looking to see if there was even anything on them or not.

I give these details not to excuse the excesses of

comic book illustration, just to explain how things like this got into print. Science fiction comics, with all the possibilities of near-naked girls, ships and aliens, bulging muscles and phallic symbols, were one of the happy hunting grounds of Dr. Wertham when he was gathering information for his book about the negative effect of comics on children. Plenty of protruding and obtruding breasts in SF comics, as well as phalanxes of pubic regions indicated with special care and attention.

Dr. Wertham's book, and the excesses of some of the comic publishers, finally dropped the curtain on this type of comic publishing for a number of years. A congressional committee—on television!—investigated the details of the horror comics. They enacted no legislation, although Great Britain did, against comics. They didn't have to. The distributors who had been financing the entire operation took a look, for a change, at just what it was they were shipping from ocean to ocean at great expense. What they saw horrified them. So they did not distribute certain titles but took them hot from the presses, stored them in warehouses for a cooling-off period—then fed them directly to the pulping machines. This fed a number of publishers to the financial pulping machines and many an artist walked the hard pavements on the way to the carwash employment agency.

The surviving publishers got the message. They joined together in a mutual castration ceremony and formed an organization called The Comics Magazine Association of America, Inc. They found an ex-New York magistrate by the name of Judge Charles F. Murphy to write up a comics code. (His name was always written that way; perhaps Judge was his first name.) All comics had to conform to the code before they could be published with the stamp of approval on the cover, and this conformance was assured by a collection of steely-eyed female virgins of advanced years. The editor would bring them the pages and then, with ink and white paint, see that crotch-bulges were taken out, cup size on breasts reduced, words excised that might give offense. Some of the proscriptions of the code make fascinating reading today.

▶65

The above is one of the grot-comics that abounded during the height of comic book publication. It is a cheap imitation of another company's successful title, adding the sex and the sadism missing from the original.

The magazines today are no longer aimed at a juvenile market—though any kiddy who picks up these is in for an interesting time! Bondage is a sophisticated adult concept, mixing sadism and masochism, all tied up in an orgasm-promoting bundle.

POUR ADULTES!
nicollet

Before censorship hit the comics everyone—even the cowboys—was getting into the horror act. Witness this typical western scene (opposite left). Home on the range indeed! The SF pulps still went one better (far right) and not satisfied with simple sadism managed, at least this once, to throw in a strong whiff of necrophilia. Why else would the bird-legged aliens want such well-preserved Earth women?

Comics, born in the United States, are now international, and European artists are breathing new life into a paralyzed and moribund art form. Esteban Maroto of Spain created a sword and sorcery character, 'Dax The Warrior' (left) evolving a new artistic style at the same time. Classic yet modern—and restrainedly sexual. The American Comics Code censors would have coronaries if presented with something like this.

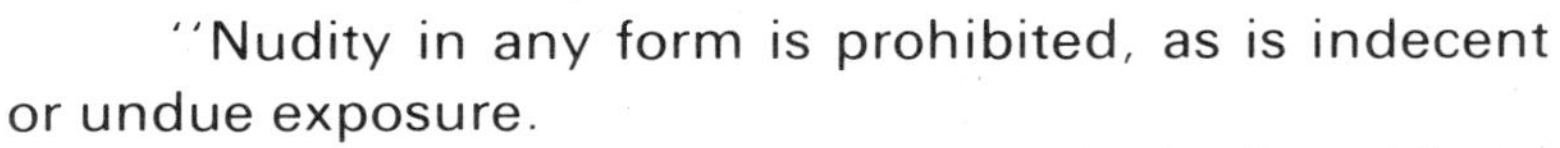

"Nudity in any form is prohibited, as is indecent or undue exposure.

"Females should be drawn realistically without exaggeration of any physical qualities.

"All scenes of horror, excessive bloodshed, gory or gruesome crimes, depravity, lust, sadism, masochism, shall not be permitted.

"Scenes dealing with, or instruments associated with walking dead, torture, vampires and vampirism, ghouls, cannibalism and werewolfism are prohibited.

"Violent love scenes as well as sexual abnormalities are unacceptable.

"Passion or romantic interest shall never be treated in such a way as to stimulate the lower and baser emotions."

Unhappily, it was never made clear just what the lower and baser emotions were. Nor what the instruments were that are associated with walking dead, vampirism or cannibalism. (Knives and forks for cannibalism?) Otherwise this list provides precise description of just what a lot of the magazines were like before the whole thing went bust. Just substitute "shall' for "shall not" and "shall never" in the code and you will have a good idea of what they contained. An excess in one direction brings an excess in the other. The comics have been whiter than white ever since, and the kids know it, and sales have never been as good again.

American comics have been overly maligned by the critics—and equally overpraised by the devotees. The truth is far more simple and drab than either extreme would have it. I find myself unmoved by the appreciators who publish books lauding the intellectual freedom and true merit of the comic medium. I was there; they can't con me. A "history" of American comics goes into spasms of joy over a certain science fiction comic, then outlines one of the tremendously "novel" stories that it published. The story was novel the first time published, but not when the plot was swiped for this comic story. I know. I supplied the SF anthologies for this publisher from which all the best plots were lifted.

▶68

BLACK
PRIESTESS
OF VARDA
TLAWED, SENTENCED TO THE
AT, A FEW FORESTERS STILL
FOUL SASSO'S
LOVELIEST WITCH!
An Exciting Novel
by ERIK FENNEL
GARSON · WELLS · SELWYN

On these two pages is exemplified the contrast between the old and the new. Here (left) we have the magnificent but old-fashioned heroine with regulation breastplates, defending herself with an old-fashioned weapon against a predictable foe who looks more like a piece of worn foam underlay than a monster. But, (this page) the artist explores a far more ambiguous relationship. Jim Burns' android is certainly a monster with his steel-bladed muscle and poison fingernails, but he's also rather sexy, and it looks as if his shapely captive thinks so too. Is that looming hardware a materialization of her own desires?

There were, and are, no good writers in comics. Just good artists. Many good writers have passed through the comics field with only a brief stop; I think of excellent SF writers and editors like H.L. Gold, Bruce Elliott and Alfred Bester. (Bruce had already abandoned comics while I was still editing them. I needed a script in a hurry and begged him to do one, just once again, but he had to refuse because he confided in me that he had sold his vomit-proof typewriter.) When good writers found themselves waist-deep in a knee-high medium they left. Comics are a very restricted field of literary endeavour and provide no future for writers whose talents seek fulfilling outlets. Not so with the artists. There are many wonderful and talented ones and I only wish that it were possible to provide better scripts for them to illustrate. This is unhappily impossible. No matter how well you decorate it, a sow's ear will never be a silk purse.

Comics are for kids. They are juvenilia. The limitations of little pictures and little blocks of words restrict the art form. Any attempt to break out of this straitjacket is limited by the realities of mass publishing and self-imposed censorship. The only way around this impasse is with underground and adult comics. They are fun, nice and dirty, and I am sure provide an important social function. More power to them, and to legitimate comic publishing as well. Write, draw, read, enjoy yourselves. Just don't keep trying to convince us of your overwhelming cultural and artistic importance.

Just as comics are not the undiscovered Rubiyat that their propagandists assure us they are—neither are they the pernicious and deadly influence that Dr. Wertham and the critics want to wish upon us. Yes, excesses in violence, sex and sadism should be considered carefully in the cinema, television—and comics. But it has been two decades since a small proportion of all the comics published featured this sort of material. You have won the battle, even the war. Comics never were much of a threat to the nation. They once exercised a little novelty and imagination and that has been successfully crushed. Go away happy and find someone else to bother.

While originality was crumbling in American comics it was bursting to life in France. Philippe Druillet draws upon the freedoms and forms of the underground comics to create his own idiom. Science fiction is the form that allows the most expression; sex and violence the most intriguing plot line. In his 'The Six Voyages of Lone Sloan' (right) he gets it all together with an explosive bang of effect.

6

Fetish for Main Course

This a field where SF art is really a winner since there is no limit to the props that can be used, therefore no limit to fetish objects.

Krafft-Ebing spelled it *fetich* and defined this widespread practice as pouring all of the sexual interest into only a part of the opposite sex. Modern psychology throws the net a bit wider and says that it is any object or part of the body that, while it need not be of a sexual nature, still causes an erotic response or fixation.

When it comes to parts of the body SF art is seen to excel. Just name your part! Breasts? Yes indeed, that is something we have always specialized in. Those brass breastplates again and all the bra-top cleavage-baring outfits that girls will apparently wear in an overheated future.

Mons Veneris? Dr. Wertham has already pointed out how insistent the comics were in careful delineation of this. The magazine illustrators don't seem to have been as active here as they should have been. As with nipples, bits of fabric and floating balls always seem to drift across at the wrong time. But a careful search will produce samples. Legs are of course prominently displayed, a veritable leg fetishist's garden of gams. Navels are in short supply but hair!—now that is something else again. A minimum of shoulder length and usually longer. The stories as well make a great play of long hair, if hair is mentioned at all. *Shambleau* by C. L. Moore is a hair-horror story. Though everyone goes around nude in S. Fowler Wright's *The World Below*, one species is completely covered with fur and the other has hair growing right down the female's back—though the men are bald as eggs. Sexual dimorphism again; we cannot escape it.

It is when we leave the body itself and get into

Vampirella (left) as drawn by the Spanish artist Enrich, can certainly be up to no good—that is in addition to her unusual dietary habits. Her outfit is a fetishist's dream of heaven; everything interesting clearly delineated, sexual suggestion explicit at all times.

inanimate objects that we observe some very interesting trends. Shoe fetishism appears to be as old as mankind; how many gallons of athlete's foot-flavored champagne have been drunk from shoes! The Chinese excelled in this, the lotus foot was made by binding the toes back, deforming them in the process, then providing a deformed shoe for the deformed foot. That's at least four different jollies rolled into one. Science fiction carries the history of shoe fetishism into the far future but shows every little imagination about its development. If a girl is not barefoot she either wears high heels or kinky boots. For a long time the men clumped around in high-laced engineer's boots (the girls too), but this changed rather quickly to a chunky ''space boot'', something like a heavy orthopedic shoe, and has remained that way.

One of the most widespread fetishes of our times will not be found mentioned at all in the works of Krafft-Ebing. No oversight this, just the march of technology bringing new and important things into our

▶76

Modern illustrations can be far more explicit (above) than was ever possible in the past. Breasts now fully revealed, but still a certain reluctance manifest concerning the mons Veneris—with a rubber glove coyly placed. A classic example of sexual dimorphism (above) is elegantly blended with the highly impractical space gear supplied for the shoe, bottom and boob brigade.

This ingenuousness, or is it obvious sensuality, is carried even further (above) where the lady's studied indifference to those clutching hands and bulging eyeballs is less than realistic.

Wow! How simple and boring the usual fetish interests of rubber boots, high heels and ventilated bras become when compared to the freedom and imagination of science fiction. No prizes given for lists of at least ten fetish objects on these pages—not to mention the jungle of penis symbols.

lives. One of the fringe benefits never suspected by B. F. Goodrich when he spilled the hot latex over the sulphur and invented vulcanizing, was the booming trade that would eventually be developed in rubber goods. Victorian fetishists had to make do with leather —and they did very well with it indeed. One prominent Victorian fell in love with gloves, (starting with his mother's, the Freudians will be happy to hear.) He liked to shake hands with as many girls as possible, and had the resulting orgasms to prove it was the glove not the hand that did it. He collected them, gloves not girls, by the thousands, slept with them, made clothes out of them in private and wore them under his own clothes in public.

But leather has declined and rubber fetishism has made great strides lately in the legalized sex shops in many countries. For a not-too-great sum one can buy aprons, girdles, hats, bras, scarves, socks, shoes—all made out of soft and desirable black rubber. These real-life substitutes can now take the place of all the rubber suits the SF heroes wore. They had to be made of rubber since they never wrinkled or tore, no matter how tough the battle. Superman always wore his into action, and Plastic Man obviously had one on made of the absolutely best in stretch fabric. (He had a lot more to answer for as well, as a glance at one of his pictures easily reveals.)

Phallic symbols might be called fetishes, but in reality serve a much more important function. The phallic symbol featured in all primitive art and was valued in life and religion until the Judeo-Christian era. To expose the male organ was considered right and not shameful up through the civilized Greeks—who put their hand over their testicles (the source of life) not their hearts when they swore an oath. It was the Romans who considered uncovered parts shameful and covered everything up. (Though they stripped slaves naked to heighten their shame.) But fashions in flashing come and go—only the potency of the phallic symbol goes on unchanged. This is the symbol of manhood, *machismo*, strength, fertility, life, continuity. It is too powerful a symbol to be put aside by changes in

Plasticman is every rubber fetishist's dream. Not only is his outfit the best rubber that money can buy—skintight and stretching and contracting for ever—but he himself is rubber with lovely, snake-like limbs. A good deal can be made of his enemies (above) with highly suggestive noses. Since fetishism is usually a solitary vice, the inability of the exhausted superman (right) to perform heterosexually has its own message.

CRASH
CLAN

ZAP
YEP

ZING

ARGH

custom. Many eastern religions feature phallic symbols, or outright giant phalli, in their rites and decoration, while western religion is a bit more subtle with serpents, fishes, church towers, mitres and such. Modern—and futuristic design permits the flourishing of phallic symbols and we have phallic automobiles, rockets and even more obvious usages.

How much of this in science fiction is purposeful and how much accidental? It is difficult to say. There are many stories of authors and artists who deliberately sought ways to get around magazine taboos. (The *Astounding* author who cracked the bad-word ban there by having one character say that his invention was, "The greatest discovery since the ball-bearing mouse-trap." "What was that?" "The tomcat.") In a few instances I know artists who drew in objects that could be interpreted in two ways. (I once wrote a script for a widely distributed comic that had an entire dictionary of taboos, and connived with the artist to sneak in a small act of rebellion. A baseball player held his bat in one hand and threw up a ball with the other. The ball was drawn just below the bat. Millions saw it and no one, including the art editor, noticed.) One artist for Ziff-Davis, while illustrating a couple fleeing through a field of giant toadstools, realized what the toadstools looked like. If you blink at the final art the escape is through a forest of gargantuan phalli.

But I think these are the exception, not the rule. Speaking as a hardworking artist and art director, I can be sure that there usually just isn't enough time to worry about items like this. Get the assignment, get the art in—and get the check. It is the old subtle subconscious that slips in most of the things we notice now. That and the swipe file. Bad artists copy good artists. Good artists use photographs and other artist's work for

The new French artists are not going to play around with any silly little subtle bits of phallic symbolism. Druillet (this page) lets it all hang out gloriously, machismo at Mach-10. Moebius (opposite page) simply abandons all pretense. Science fiction art has finally come of age.

The rocket ship is still the most potent phallic symbol and for once (left) its use has been deliberate. The sword and sorcery art makes great use of its swords, usually with a bit more subtlety than below. Though of course the French (opposite page) have abandoned pretense completely—and humorously.

details of costume, architecture, machinery and such. Since the future has not arrived yet new SF artists turn to the older ones for details. In this manner artistic clichés are perpetuated. Occasionally artists, such as Kelly Freas in his *Planet Stories* covers, would deliberately do artistic parodies of cliché covers. This did not happen very often. In most artwork, particularly commercial art, what you see is what the artist wants you to see. Subtlety and symbolism will have to be read in by the viewer. Ninety-nine per cent of the time the artist was conscious of doing no more than providing the piece of art asked for.

ALL NEW! A SPECIAL EPIC!
THE CATACLYSMIC CONCLUSION OF
CONAN THE CONQUEROR

7

Is Conan Dating Clark Kent?

The evidence will have to be examined very closely, the art analyzed, and a decision carefully reached before we can even talk about homosexuality in science fiction. Certainly it does not exist in the stories! I am sure that Kimball Kinnison, the Lensman who symolizes the muscular space opera school of SF, would rather become a hated zwilnik before he would lay a friendly hand on a shipmate's bottom. Hetero is okay, and in this direction the word love can even be mentioned, the occasional chaste embrace or kiss described. But not the others! Shiploads of virile men would blast around the galaxy, sealed together for years in a spaceship, with never a hint of a nocturnal emission—not to say a loving embrace. Early science fiction Just Did Not Mention Those Things.

With a single exception. Conan the Conqueror, the Barbarian from the North, the fearless, crushing, fighting man. The sexiest pig to whom women are just chattels to be diddled and discarded. Conan, and his creator Robert E. Howard, offer the grandest opportunities for symbolism, analysis and second guessing that could be imagined. It was years after Howard's death in 1936 before the real Conan popularity began and it shows no sign of slowing yet. There is an organization, The Hyborian Legion, that dotes on the master's works. His stories have been collected, unfinished ones completed by other writers, and new ones written by L. Sprague deCamp and Lin Carter. The Conan cult, though it began in science fiction, like Star Trek fandom, is now big enough to enjoy a separate existence of its own. Conan's adventures are referred to as "sword-and-sorcery" and many other novels of this type have been written and published. Conan fans publish fanzines dedicated to Hyborian matters—Conan was born in the mythical land of Hyboria—and the oldest and best of these is *Amra*. It is most professionally edited and produced, and catholic enough in its approach to its favorite form of fiction to print an article about the darker, sexual side of Conan's nature. The article produced a surge of correspondence and, lo and behold, one of the letters was from our friend Frederic Wertham, MD. The doctor makes a number of interesting points, although some of them are so committedly Freudian that only another Freudian would agree completely. But he does clearly state what he feels is Conan's sexual drive.

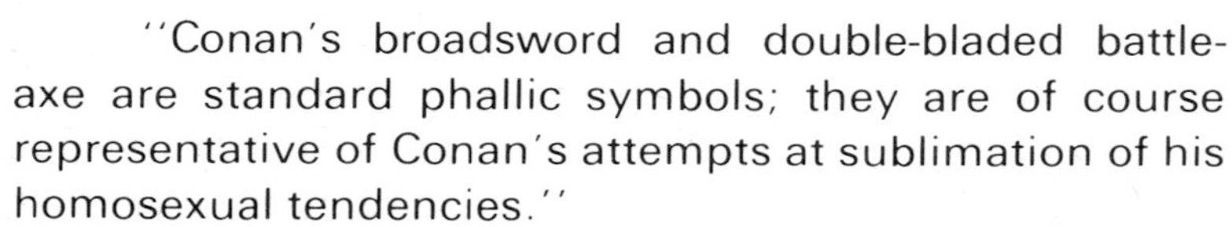

"Conan's broadsword and double-bladed battle-axe are standard phallic symbols; they are of course representative of Conan's attempts at sublimation of his homosexual tendencies."

There, he has gone and said it. The most virile hero in science fiction is as queer as a nine dollar bill. However, as much as I value a good deal of the doctor's psychological arguments, I think that he has absolutely no future as a literary critic. He writes of the author of the Conan series thus:

"Howard, a thorough writer capable of much subtlety, has given us still more guideposts to lead us to the proper conclusions ... I'm certain that Howard would not have wanted our knowledge of Conan's deviant sexuality to make us think less of Conan."

Oh, really? I would think that a not-too close read of the Conan stories, along with other horror and fantasy stories Howard wrote, would reveal that subtlety is one thing they just do not have. Howard believed in his hero. I am afraid that a chance for a good Freudian

analysis of the writer was missed here. Yes indeed, caves are accepted symbols of female genitals, so that Conan's constant lurking in caves and rushing about in them certainly could relate to his undoubted Oedipus complex and resultant homosexuality. But I tend to believe that this relates more to the author's own life.

Robert Ervin Howard spent his entire life in the small town of Cross Plains, Texas. He was small and much put upon as a boy, but later worked hard at body-building until he was over two hundred pounds of solid muscle. Yet he never left home, hated his father, adored his possessive mother so much that, at the age of thirty, he still lived with her. Nor did he have any girl-friends. When his mother was in a terminal coma with cancer, Howard took a Colt. 38 and blew his brains out.

Howard did identify with his hero, Conan, and admitted as much many times. When Dr. Wertham writes that ''A basic knowledge of Freudian symbolism reveals still more of Conan's psychological complications, ''We can agree completely. But I find it hard to agree when he insists that this was all done consciously by the author. Conan is a crypto-homosexual and the entire school of sword-and-sorcery reflects this fact. Other than the proliferation of Freudian symbolism in the magazine art there seems to be no other trace of homosexuality. (Though the art is good enough. What *can* one think when seeing Conan chained in a

From the pages of 'Amra' (opposite and above) come some of the most revealing and openly suggestive illustrations. There is no doubt what the sword—or the snake—stands for. An underground comic parodies Conan with a strip called 'Gonad the Horney' which says it all.

The muscle cult of heroes has even been organised (following page) into something called 'Superheroes'. This title makes as much sense as the advertising slogan 'whiter than white'. Grouping them like this removes any viability they might have as individuals. The Druillet hero (following pages, opposite) has a grimmer reality.

dungeon being menaced by an eighty foot long snake!) But if the magazine science fiction art is pristine, the same cannot be said of the comic SF art. To reassure ourselves that we are not reading too much into what could be the total happenings of chance, let us turn to Dr. Wertham again and see what he has to say. As a senior psychiatrist in the New York City Department of Hospitals, he should have been able to spot any small deviations from the norm.

''Only someone ignorant of the fundamentals of psychiatry and of the psychopathology of sex can fail to realize a subtle atmosphere of homoeroticism which pervades the adventures of the mature 'Batman' and his young friend 'Robin'.''

All right, let's look. It is going to have to be subtleties because I will swear that Batman never laid a hand upon Robin in public. Well, not quite true. They do drag each other from danger fairly often, and occasionally carry the other when unconscious. And, yes, B does occasionally put a friendly arm around R in the security of their home. Their sybaritic pad must surely have put a gleam in Dr. Wertham's eye. Luxury, soft furniture, warm and cosy, with both occupants well dressed at all times, surrounded by good things to eat and drink, without financial worries since B is a millionaire. R is his ''ward'' and if a reader, like the good doctor, were to see only this set-up as I have just described it—why it could be assumed that you could read ''bumboy'' for ''ward'' and let it go at that.

But this not all there is to it. In the beginning was

Yes, homosexuality can be read into the relationships between heroes and their boy companions. All those muscles and tight underwear—and being carried away like this (above). The case has yet to be proven. The argument is far stronger—as are the swords—(right) for a strong homosexual element in sword and sorcery.

Bruce Wayne, a nice young millionaire playboy whose parents are killed by criminals. So, though he now still plays by day, at night he slips into his avenging bat outfit and goes out and avenges. When this strip became popular, the killing was toned down and Dick Grayson was introduced for young readers to identify with. Dick was also orphaned by hoods and, since his parents were acrobats and he was part of the act, he is ready to start bouncing around rooftops as Robin, the Boy Wonder. All clean-cut and healthy, you see.

The Human Torch and his good little mate, Toro, perhaps offer more clues to a possible hidden relationship. Fire itself stands for sex as when Milton writes, "That burning mentioned by St. Paul, whereof Marriage ought to be the remedy." This dynamic duo fight by throwing fire-balls; read what you will into that. They wear the usual rubber clothing that reveals and conceals at the same time. And again the difference in age and virility. But once again a study of the comic's history reveals something interesting. The Human Torch isn't human at all—but an android built for the job. Homosexual androids are a little hard to accept.

This same pattern is seen in other comics of this type, where a man of unusual powers has a boy assistant, such as Captain America and Bucky. A lot can be read into this kind of relationship—but a lot of this depends upon who is doing the reading. Dr. Wertham reports that a practising homosexual knew perfectly well what Batman and Robin were up to. If this person were shown a pound jar of Vaseline he would know what it is used for too. But on the other hand an instrument technician would know it is for delicate ball-bearing races where it is the lubricant of choice.

I take this case as strong—but unproven. In a court of law there would be reasonable doubt, so the vice squad can't bust Batman yet. But stay out of public toilets, Batman! They'll get you by entrapment if they can't do it any other way.

Even though Batman "... often stands with his legs spread, the genital region discreetly evident", as Dr. Wertham says, this classic pose is one passed on from hero to hero by countless artists. I think Occam's razor will work well here. A big hero to do big things, a boy companion for the boy readers to identify with. Once the pattern was started all the dim writers simply copied. They lack subtlety in everything else so I cannot think them capable of subtlety in as serious a matter as sex.

However there is a far stronger case against Wonder Woman and her merry band of girls. This time I think that the *Psychiatric Quarterly* has better reasons than the ones Dr. Wertham has used against leg-spreading Batman. They write about Wonder Woman as "... a series ... which portrays extremely sadistic hatred of all males in a framework which is plainly lesbian."

The girls, in their tight and revealing outfits, do whip, strap, tie and generally humiliate men in this strip. While at the same time saying things like "If you are naughty I'll see you get no candy for a week." This is pretty strong stuff and this might be a lesbian band at that. But *Psychiatric Quarterly* seems unaware that Wonder Woman was created to the publisher's orders for a female superhero with whom young girl readers could identify. The idea was originated and the first scripts written by William Moulton Marston—who was a psychologist. Unless Marston was a sick psychologist and wrote the lesbian bit on purpose to pervert the world, *Psychiatric Quarterly* and Dr. Wertham are very far off base.

When the evidence is added up I think that Conan is the only possible pansy in the science fiction garden of roses, and this done completely inadvertently by the author who would have been shocked and horrified at the suggestion. There is plenty of sex of all other kinds in our imaginative dreamland but, at the moment, I see no particularly strong evidence of the presence of this particular sort.

8

The Chains Cast Off...

And then science fiction, with plots theoretically set in the far future, finally entered the twentieth century. Sexually, that is. And the moment in time can be pinpointed exactly.

July, 1952.

Volume 27, Number 1 of *Startling Stories*, edited by Samuel Mines. This was the August issue of the magazine, since the cover date on American monthly magazines is when they go off sale, not on. It contained a story by Philip José Farmer titled *The Lovers*. It was Farmer's first published story—more power to him for writing it. And equal applause to Mines for publishing it. *The Lovers* is a well told and moving story of a man from Earth who encounters, and loves, a female alien who resembles a woman—although she is in reality a form of symbiotic insect that adopts human form. The illustration was commonplace and the story far less shocking than its critics would have us believe. Here is Farmer describing the mating of man and alien, the shocking copy that rocked the entire science fiction nation at the time.

" . . . And love me. I'll love you, Hal, and we'll not see the world outside nor need to. For the time being. Forget in my arms."

"They drank the purplish liquor. After a while he picked her up and carried her into the bedroom. There he forgot. The only disconcerting thing was that she insisted upon keeping her eyes open, even during the climax, as if she were trying to photograph his features upon her mind."

The reaction, in the little world of science fiction, was just what might have been expected. The traditionalists, the pulp-orientated readers who wanted no changes in the stone age style and content that they worshipped, were most annoyed. They were very much in a minority. The greater proportion of the magazine readers simply accepted the story without protest for, in relation to literary sex outside of SF, it was pretty mild stuff. The discerning readers and fans applauded the story and the doors that it might open for an adult treatment of sex in science fiction.

Virgil Finlay did the illustration for Farmer's story 'The Lovers' when it first appeared in 1952. Well drawn, but containing only a strong hint as to the nature of the story. It took almost 25 years more for the chains to be finally cast off. Now Richard Corben (following pages, left) and Philippe Druillet (following page, right) can show us the lovers in close proximity at last. How refreshing the reality is after all the hints, winks, nudges and smirks.

Although the time was ripe the response was not immediate. There was no flood of realistic sex stories in the magazines. The editors would surely not have printed them but, what is more important, the writers were not writing them. They weren't ready. The occasional, exceptional writer was. In 1953 Theodore Sturgeon published a story titled *The World Well Lost*. Here the traditional spaceship is crewed untraditionally by two men who relate and operate within a most complicated homosexual bond. The writer was once more ahead of his audience. Sturgeon says; "I wrote an emphatic sort of tale about homosexuals, and my mailbox filled up with cards drenched with scent and letters written in purple ink with green capitals." The true SF fans however rejected the story.

These stories stood alone for a long time. The first dribble of water through the dike does not let in the entire ocean. Pulp taboos and pulp thinking still ruled. Writers and editors still operated within the old limitations. And it was not only sex that was taboo. Ten years later I wrote a story with an atheist as hero, *The Streets of Ashkelon*, which was instantly rejected by every SF magazine in the United States. Later it was published in England and there were no riots in the streets. (It was eventually anthologized and published in the United States and recently included in a high school text there. So things do change, albeit slowly.) There is an inertia against change that writers have to fight against constantly; the automatic acceptance of the status quo. Forward looking as science fiction is, it still shares this disability. Stories are, after all, just little specks of ink on wood pulp. A writer looks at a piece of blank paper, then impresses it with words. The writer's attitudes, to himself and the world, shape the words and the stories he produces. If the writer thinks of himself as a pulp writer, he will produce only pulp ideas in pulp language, while carefully avoiding all the taboo pulp topics. In the fifties the older authors were trained pulp authors and never considered moving outside the limitations they had always worked with. The second generation authors, the ones who grew up reading the pre- and post-war science fiction, also had this pulp orientation when they began writing. They were fans turned writers and produced their stories in the traditions on which they had been weaned.

Farmer was in the forefront of the third generation of writers. He knew and enjoyed his SF—but read and enjoyed other forms of literature as well. (In his personal library there exists what is perhaps the world's largest collection of *The Odyssey* in different languages.) Third generation writers look upon SF as a tool that they can use to express their ideas. It is not the be-all and end-all of the dedicated fan writer.

However in the early fifties the giants of the third generation, like Thomas M. Disch, Michael Moorcock and Norman Spinrad, were not yet in their teens. Any advances had to be made by the old lags who had the insight to see beyond the restrictions on which they had been raised.

Yet no matter what works of avant-garde art a writer produces, they are worthless unless an editor is there who will recognize their qualities and publish them. All credit then to Mines who, in a pure pulp magazine, published *The Lovers*. There were two other editors then who would be more receptive to change in science fiction. In 1950 the first issue of *Galaxy Science Fiction* appeared, edited by Horace Gold, followed by *The Magazine of Fantasy and Science Fiction* in 1951, edited by Anthony Boucher. Both individualistic, both fine writers as well as editors, both were to add new dimensions to science fiction, which, in reality, had changed very little since the Campbell Revolution in 1936. Campbell took one step sideways and did his thing in *Astounding*. All of the other magazines did the same old thing, ringing the changes yet one more time. It took two new magazines and two new editors to add other dimensions.

F & SF, as it soon became known when the jawbreaker of the original title became cumbersome, specialized in what can only be called decent writing. Boucher, a man of great taste and wit, made no attempt to draw a fine line between fantasy and science fiction. He wanted novel ideas that did not necesarily belong in one category or another. He wanted them

written well and encouraged writers, both old and new, to do their absolute best. They rose to the challenge.

Galaxy brought the realization to science fiction that there are more sciences than the traditional hard ones of chemistry and physics. Psychology, anthropology, archaeology—even demography were seen as legitimate areas of literary endeavour. Psychiatry featured large as well. And, occasionally, a hint of sex did appear. Unhappily, in this single aspect, both editors still had pulp reflexes. (Though not in their personal lives where their interests were widespread. Boucher, one of the wittiest of men, had a copy of G. Legman's definitive book *The Limerick* shipped to him from France—and ended up in terrible trouble with the post office because of this. A crime! I have before me now an English paperback edition which is on sale everywhere. Things *do* change for the better, if ever so slowly.) What both editors did do was to encourage writers to expand their literary muscles, to enter new areas of writing, to think better of themselves and their field.

The first magazine to make any concerted attempt to break the pulp sex barrier was *Venture Science Fiction*. It ran all of ten issues in 1957 and 1958, then was knackered along with a lot of other magazines when the SF boomlet collapsed. It was edited by Robert P. Mills, a professional editor of many years' experience, now a literary agent. He never particularly asked for sexy SF. He just let it be known that he had no taboos at all and what could the writer bring him that was interesting? This relaxed attitude led to his publishing many fine stories, both with and without sex, and it is a shame the magazine died before it reached its full strength.

Although the magazines were beginning to face up to the fact that sex really existed, the book publishers knew that it did not and saw to it that none appeared on the shelves of this always pristine literature. But the writers were ready, and perhaps the very first novel that respected sex as a normal part of the human condition was *Non-Stop* by Brian W. Aldiss, which was published in 1958. It was his first novel and it definitely was *not* in the pulp SF tradition. Nor was it about sex. It is an adult, literarily sound novel, written

as well or better than most mainstream novels acclaimed by the critics, where the characters live well-rounded and complete lives. Sex is part of everyone's life and so it is in this novel. Not forced in, nor dragged in with a smirk, not inserted to titillate moronic readers. Just part of life. The hero, Complain, is beset by numerous problems and only one of them is his desire for sex, to forget his other problems for even a brief moment. There is a certain book that is most important to the story and it is brought in in the following manner:

"She sat down on the bed. As Complain sat beside her, she unbuttoned her tunic and pulled out a narrow black book, handing it to him. It was warm from her body heat. Dropping it, he put his hand on her blouse, tracing the arable contours of her breasts."

And that is as far as it goes here. The girl cares more about the book, she is not interested now in his advances, the story goes on. But we know more about this unhappy man; we share his frustration. The scene develops the story and the characterization. It is normal and natural and not smut at all. Many years were to pass before other writers would be able to realize this ideal in science fiction. Most never will; pulp rules too firmly.

It would be nice to say that illustration also became more liberal as the stories tested new grounds. Unhappily it did not. The package was still the same. The rockets roared and the brazen bras dazzled and all looked very much as it always had.

Except for a single very unusual experiment by World Editions, the publishers of *Galaxy*, to sell good cheese as cheap chalk. In one way this was in the noble tradition of SF where the art suggested far more than was ever realized inside. *Planet Stories* specialized in this, promising everything, including fellatio, on their covers. If the art wasn't enough of a hard sell they jazzed up the story titles, taking Theodore Sturgeon's cover story, the original title has long been lost—even to the author and retitling it *The Incubi of Parallel X*. They were not the only magazine to play the mislabeling game. The first edition of *Two Complete Science-*

Adventure Books, magazine titles were better in the old days, features Isaac Asimov's *Pebble in the Sky*. The story of an old Jewish tailor whisked into the future and what happens to him there. What did *not* happen to him was what was seen on the cover where concupiscent hero and heroine blast away with ray guns.

Galaxy Science Fiction Selected Novels did far better than that. Look at *Mars Child* by Cyril Judd (the pen name for the collaboration of Cyril Kornblith and Judy Merrill) which *Galaxy* originally published as a serial. A sort of frontier story in space, where settlers on Mars are analogous to settlers on the western frontier. Filled with greed, and the hopes of conning oversexed youths out of their precious money, the publishers issued it as a paperback entitled *Sin in Space* with a cover featuring a disrobing girl and a smirking spaceman. (He is wearing spacesuit and helmet which should have made things a little difficult.) Not satisfied with this success they also published *Odd John* by Olaf Stapledon in the same series. They did not change the title but rather enhanced any possible double meanings of it by showing John looking exceedingly odd, particularly about the eyes, stalking in the nude a nude girl whose charms are only partly concealed by a fortuitous piece of driftwood. This does not *quite* illustrate the gentle, kindly superman theme of the book.

This was all that the fifties, and even the early sixties, had to offer for the most part. The authors occasionally enjoyed the burgeoning liberality, with books such as Theodore Sturgeon's *Venus Plus X* in 1960, which is about a hermaphrodite human society, but the art did not reflect this.

However change was in the air.

9

...The Gates Thrown Wide

The world changed. Consenting adults had always done things together, with each other's consent, but only in the sixties did they begin to do it legally. Hardcore porn, that used to be sold from under the counter, now had its own little section in the book stores. *Playboy,* always in the front with things sexual, broke the photographic beaver barrier and permitted female pubic hair to be shown in their picture sections. Thus ending the illusion, shared by millions of American boys, that girls were as smooth as billiard balls ''Down There''. While breasts have been prominent in photographs in American mass circulation magazines for years, there was an unwritten agreement that pubic hair could never be shown. It was always carefully airbrushed out. (When I was art director for some nasty little magazines that featured pics of this type, we used to apply water with the fingertip when these pictures came back from the engraver. This removed the airbrush paint and the nude photograph looked much better on the wall.) Magazines became more and more

specific about sex and were available everywhere; the only ban on their sale apparently being a height barrier since they were placed only on the top shelves in the shops. Supposedly, I imagine, because children are shorter than adults and couldn't reach them. (Making life interesting for very tall young boys and hell for mature midgets.)

The cinema really made the most of this new liberality by permitting the showing of hardcore skin-flicks like *Deep Throat* to audiences of Adults Over 21. This also generated the new vice of cinematic voyeurism. I have never seen this mentioned in the medical texts though I have observed it at California drive-ins with low fences. Libidinous and impoverished motorists would park outside and watch the class X films without hearing the sound-track, which might be, perhaps, an improvement.

The world was filled with sex, ready for sex, enjoyed sex. Sex in films and sex in books made money. But was the world ready for sex in science fiction?

The answer is no. Some sexy SF novels were published—collectors items now—but this practice soon stopped. Apparently there were two different audiences. The films were more successful, *Barbarella* being the best example, *Flesh Gordon* perhaps the worst. How much of this rejection was the fault of the writers, the readers or the publishers is arguable. But it just did not click in the United States. I know the publishers were at least partially to blame. Well before the new liberality had filtered down to science fiction I prepared an anthology of sexy science fiction. It wasn't *that* sexy, culled as it was from current and past magazines and books. The working title was *Starship 69*, which certainly identified the contents. It went to every publisher in New York and was turned down by every publisher, including one major paperback house that was churning out a line of hardcore porn from the cubicle next to the one where my editor found my anthology too hot to handle. Doublethink. You just don't mix sex and science fiction. Though you can mix sex and comics, and even mix in grass, hash, drugs and comics. The underground comics came out of the underground press which came out of the Vietnam war, and were one of the protests against that singularly vile bit of butchery. Since there was no way protesters could get into print they had to publish their own newspapers to attempt to tell the United States that something had gone badly wrong. The first was the *East Village Other* which began in 1965. By 1966 there were at least four other papers being published across the country—and all of them used art and comic

Inside front cover for 'American Flier' (opposite)—above ground, underground comic; SF and sex blending again. Nice piece of symbolism for the naked angel (above)—from the French of course.

art to tell a story. The next step was obviously a complete underground comic book. The first ones were badly printed and badly drawn, until *Zap* appeared in 1968. Written and drawn by Robert Crumb, the leading underground artist, it was soon followed by *Despair, Big Ass* and *Slow Death Funnies.*

These do not sound like comics that might be approved by the comics code authority, and they are, in many ways, certainly a reaction against the simple-minded authority rules. A number of them bore varyingly obscene imitations of the code's own seal of approval. Here at last was anti-establishment comics that featured sex as a commonplace, encouraged opposition to drug prohibition and pushed other liberal causes. Here science fiction rode high, the natural field of escapist endeavour. The underground comics are a healthy and natural reaction against a stultifying and destructive national mood and serve many an important function. Unhappily, they are all so badly drawn that much of the effect has been lost.

▶110

TES VRAIS YEUX...TA BOUCHE !C'EST DEGOUTANT ET TELLEMENT FASCINANT...

JE VEUX AUSSI VOIR TES YEUX!

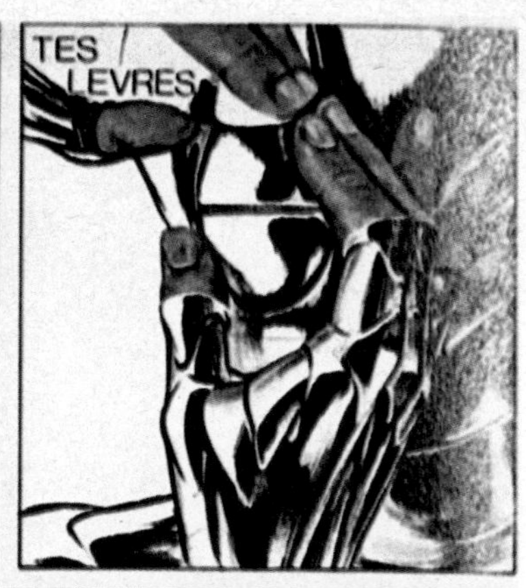
TES LEVRES

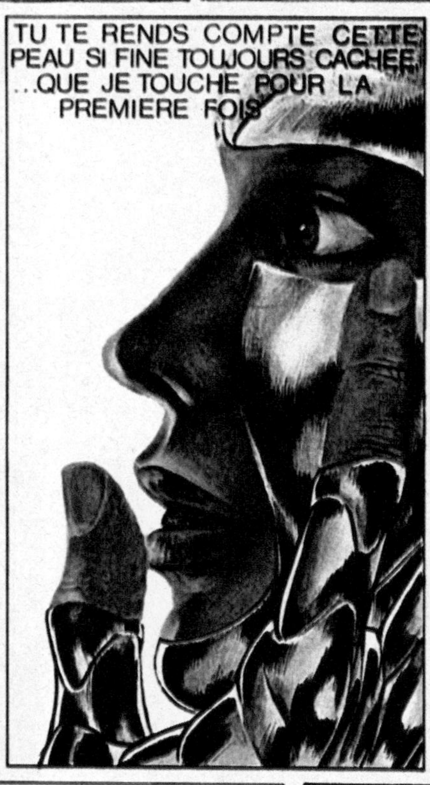
TU TE RENDS COMPTE CETTE PEAU SI FINE TOUJOURS CACHEE ...QUE JE TOUCHE POUR LA PREMIERE FOIS

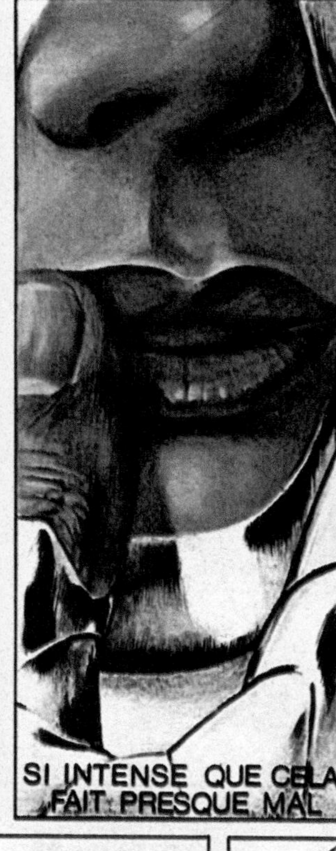
SI INTENSE QUE CELA FAIT PRESQUE MAL

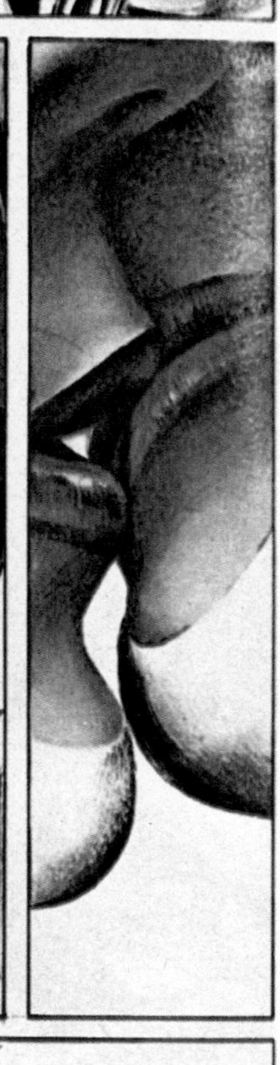

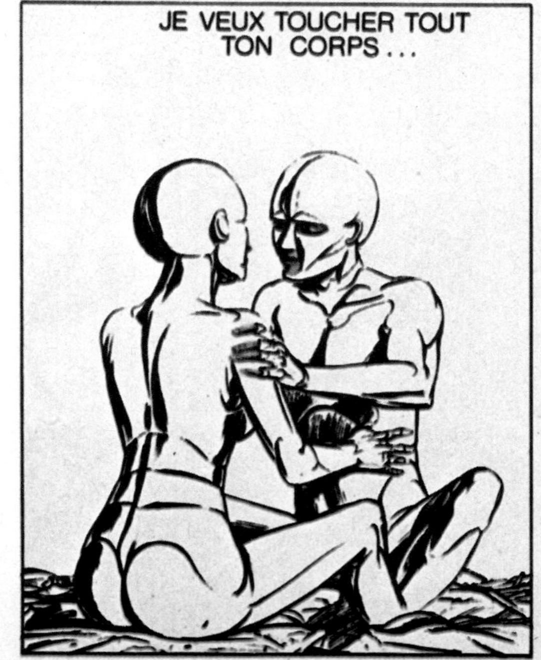
JE VEUX TOUCHER TOUT TON CORPS...

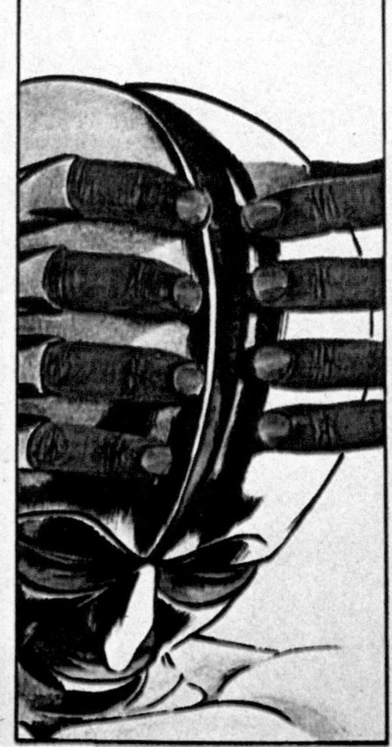

This is a particularly elegant strip from 'Metal Hurlant'. A man and woman encased in protective metal in a hostile world rediscover their own sensuality, but in doing so risk death.

(Previous pages) The Spanish artist Esteban Maroto again, with a stream of the sword and sorcery fantasy he does so well. It has enough naked women, wizards, monsters, angels and warriors to people the most exotic of dreams.
(These pages) The French magazine 'Fume c'est du Macedo' is modern, specific and wonderfully illustrated. The golden Venus (left) shows an ideal of science fiction woman-hood, concurring remarkably with Botticelli's 500 year old goddess.

KESSELRING EDITEUR

Genuine femlib, even among the monsters, although her victim is not quite as tender as his.

It took the foreigners to show us how life, art, sex and science fiction could be blended into an exciting new experience.

Comics have been around a long time and they are popular the world over. American comics are well known in a number of countries, The Phantom being one of the characters with the biggest international following. The names change (Flash Gordon becomes Jens Lyn—Jens Lightning—in Denmark) and the characters show a unique linguistic ability, but the stories remain the same. In addition to translations, there are various national comics that just don't export. They are *fumetti* in Italian—"little smokes", meaning the balloons issuing from the characters mouths—and they and other Latins enjoy as well saccharine romances that are comprised of still photographs, not drawings. There are comic artists in different countries, excellent ones who are at times far superior to our American and British ones. Publishers in both these countries have been using Spanish and Italian artists for years because of the excellent quality of their work.

But comics were still comics up until quite recently when the French invented a whole new ball game.

Comic fandom is international. Collectors all around the world treasure American comics, as well as their own, and there are countless magazines, both amateur and professional, dedicated to this hobby. So in darkest France people were reading comics, collecting comics, thinking about comics. Until something magical happened.

These new creations are not comics. They are out of comics, certainly, but are inspired as much by cinematic technique and fine art. Calling them adult comics is to diminish them. I prefer to think of them as a new art form, so new that it does not have a title as yet. Stories in illustration is correct, but clumsy. Perhaps we should adapt and internationalize an appropriate term just as science fiction has become the correct term in every language except Italian, where *fantascienza* is used, a title better than the original in many ways.

'Big Apple' (above) New York's own sexy underground comic with its own brand of SF on the cover. Tousle the Super Android (right) has built Steeleye, superstud and machismo-man—read all the sexual symbolism into this that you want . . .

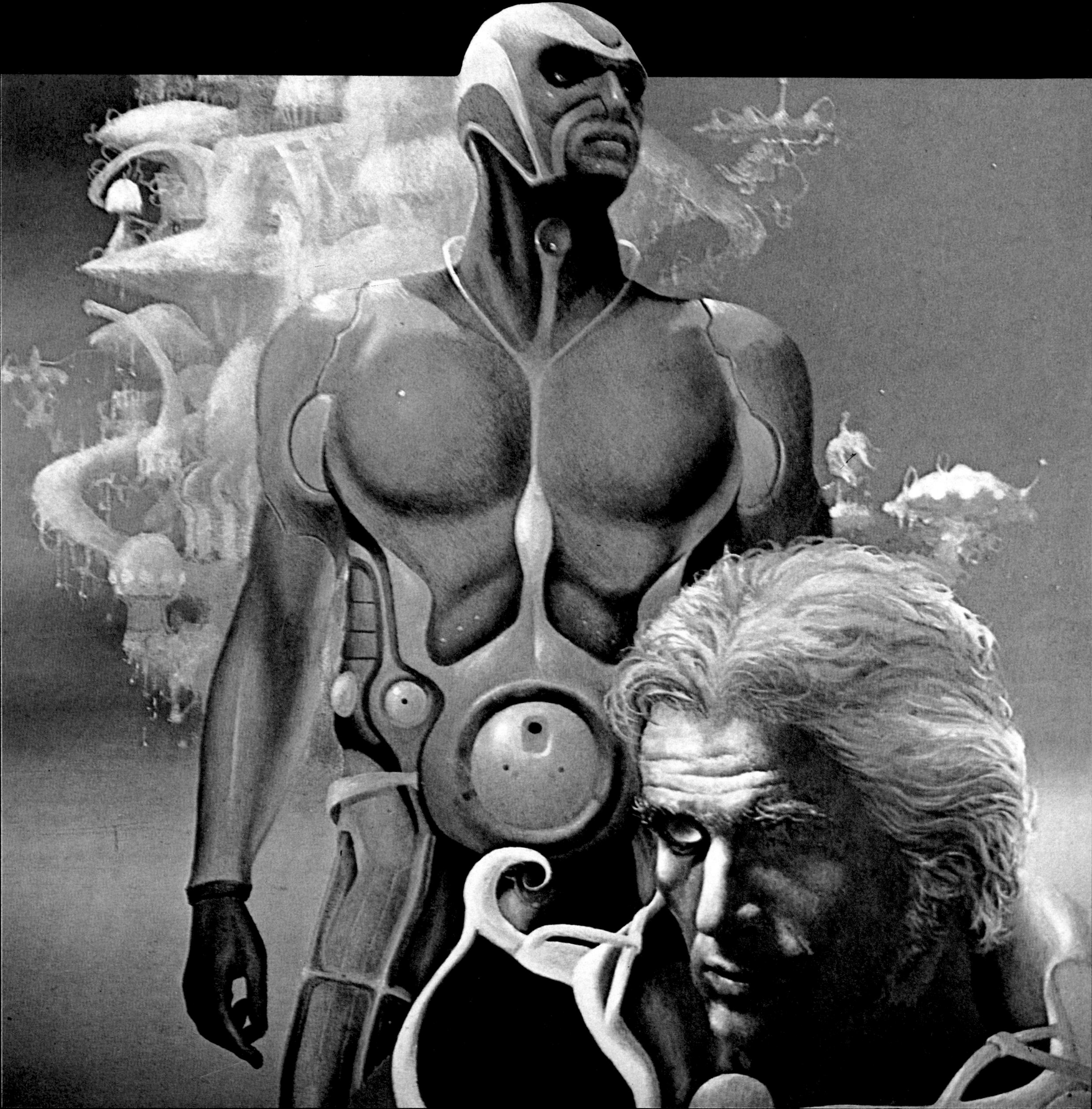

Girl in an alien forest eats of the phallic fruit and becomes impregnated by something strange . . .

The underground comics in the United States and the stories in illustration in France have vitalized and changed the standard image of comics. Ordinary comics, as published in the United States, are at a dead end. Bad stories illustrated in a stylized manner, which is rapidly becoming a fossilized manner. They are juvenilia and, without major changes as heralded in France, will always remain that way.

In the meantime there is something new in the world, a new art form that has grown out of the older forms. I think it is wonderful and inspiring and I long to work in it myself. Its candid and realistic approach towards sex is a breath of fresh air that might, hopefully, blow away all memory of the evil Comics Code Authority.

''Nudity in any form is prohibited.'' Oh no it's not—it is here in all its glory.

''Females shall be drawn realistically without exaggeration of any physical qualities.'' Not any more, Judge Murphy. What was good enough for stone age and bronze age man is good enough for us. Breasts that span the world, that's what we need more of. Lingams like sequoias to refertilize the world of art!

Looking at these pictures I think we have finally reached Maturity in science fiction art. It has been a long hard battle, with the writing rushing ahead of the art for years. If the battle is not won it is at least in its final stages and I think we can see the end in sight.

I am particularly proud that science fiction, the literature of unbound imagination, should have fostered art that is just as free.

I look forward to seeing more and more of it.

And this was all Buck Rogers gave you in the old days, a phallic rocketship.
On the opposite page, a cool look to the future.

RESTAURANT
BEER

COLOUR PLATE ARTISTS

- **6** — F. ANDERSON, *Planet Stories March 1951*
- **11** — RIBERA, *Circus no 7*
- **14** — EARLE K. BERGEY, *Thrilling Wonder June 1943*; *Monsters Unleashed*
- **18** — SANJULIAN, *Warren Calendar 1977*
- **19** — SOLE, *Metal Hurlant 3*
- **22** — EARLE K BERGEY, *Startling Stories Spring 1944*; N. SAUNDERS, *Super Science Stories March 1950*; EARLE K. BERGEY, *Startling Stories*
- **23** — N. ADAMS, *L'Echo des Savanes no 19*
- **26** — FRANK KELLY FREAS, *Planet Stories Nov 1953*
- **27** — EARLE K. BERGEY, *Planet Stories May 1951*; LEO MOREY, *Science Fiction Quarterly Aug 1951*
- **30** — F. ANDERSON, *Planet Stories Nov 1950*
- **31** — MILTON LUROS, *Future Science Nov 1950*; SANJULIAN, *Warren Calendar 1977*
- **34** — MOEBIUS, *Metal Hurlant 6*
- **35** — VOSS, *Metal Hurlant 10*
- **38** — SANJULIAN, *Warren Calendar 1977*
- **42** — EARLE K. BERGEY, *Startling Stories Jan 1950*
- **43** — R. M. BULL, *Science Fantasy Winter 1951-52*
- **46** — ED. EMSH, *Galaxy S F Sept 1954*
- **47** — HUBERT ROGERS, *Astounding Oct 1939*
- **50** — JEAN-MICHEL NICOLLET, *Metal Hurlant 8*
- **54** — F. ANDERSON, *Planet Stories Fall 1948*
- **55** — F. ANDERSON, *Planet Stories Winter 1949*; F. ANDERSON, *Action Stories no 4*
- **58** — FRANK KELLY FREAS, *Planet Stories May 1954*
- **59** — EARLE K. BERGEY, *Startling Stories March 1942*; HARRY HARRISON, *Beware March no 14*
- **62** — JOHN WILLIE, *The Adventures of Sweet Gwendoline 1946*

63
JEAN-MICHEL NICOLLET
Metal Hurlant 5

66
F. ANDERSON
Planet Stories Winter 1947

67
JIM BURNS
3 Eyes (novel)

70
ENRICH
Vampirella Calendar 1977

74
VIRGIL FINLAY
Future Science Fiction June 1959
EARLE K. BERGEY
Startling Stories Sept 1949

75
GEORGE TORJUSSEN
Devilina Vol 1 no 2
SANJULIAN
Warren Calendar 1977

78
DRUILLET
Lone Sloane, Dargaud Editeur

79
MOEBIUS
Metal Hurlant 5

82
BORIS
Conan no 10

86
ALEX TOTH
Marvel Superfriends

87
DRUILLET
Lone Sloane, Dargaud Editeur

90
RICHARD CORBEN
Fantagor

94
RICHARD CORBEN
Metal Hurlant 6

95
DRUILLET
Xragael, Dargaud Editeur

98
MACEDO
Les Fume ces du Macedo

99
SANJULIAN
Warren Calendar 1977

102/3
FRANCOIS SCHUITEN
Metal Hurlant 13

106
MACEDO
Circus no 5

107
MACEDO
Les Fume ces du Macedo

110
Stu Schwatzberg, Larry Hama
Paul Kirchner, Wallace Wood
Big Apple

111
JIM BURNS
Steeleye (novel)

114
DICK CALKINS
Buck Rogers

115
ROMAIN SLOCOMBE
Metal Hurlant 8

ACKNOWLEDGEMENTS

Thanks and acknowledgements to the following:

F. Anderson: 6, 30, 54, 55, 66; Ribera, Circus: 11; Tardi, Metal Hurlant: 12, 13, 41; Earle K. Bergey: 14, 22, 27, 42, 59, 74; Marvel Comics: 14; Sanjulian: 18, 31, 38, 75, 99; Sole, Metal Hurlant: 19; Selecciones Illustradas: 20; N. Saunders: 22; N. Adams: 23; Alex Raymond: 24, 25; Dick Calkins: 25, 114; Frank Kelly Freas: 26, 58; Leo Morey: 27; Milton Luros: 31, 97; Macedo: 32, 33, 49, 98, 106/7; Moebius, Metal Hurlant: 34, 44/5, 79; Viss, Metal Hurlant: 35; Corben, Metal Hurlant: 37, 94; R.M. Bull: 43; Ed. Emsh: 46; Hubert Rogers: 47; Jean-Michel Nicollet, Metal Hurlant: 51, 63; Barney Steel: 53; Hannes Bok: 33, 56; Jeff Jones: 57; alex, Metal Hurlant: 58; Harry Harrison: 59; Eneg, Metal Hurlant: 60, 62; John Willie, Bizarre Publishing Co: 62; Esteban Maroto: 64, 104/5; Jim Burns: 67, 111; Druillet, Dargaud Editeur: 69, 78, 81, 87, 88, 95; Enrich: 70; Virgil Finlay: 74, 92; George Torjussen, Seaboard Periodicals: 75; James Cawthorn, Amra: 80, 84; Boris, Marvel Comics Inc: 82; George Barr: 84; Raul Garcia Capella: 85; Alex Toth: 86; Richard Corben, Fantagor: 90; American Flyer, Print Mint, Inc: 100; Larry Welz, Larry Sutherland & Larry Todd: 100; Denis Sire, Metal Hurlant: 101; Francois Schuiten, Metal Hurlant: 102/3; Russ Heath: 108/9; Flo Steinberg & Big Apple Productions: 110; Stu Schwatzberg, Larry Hama, Paul Kirchner, Wallace Wood: 110; Caza, Metal Hurlant: 112/3; Romain Slocombe, Metal Hurlant: 115; D. C. Comics.

Special Thanks to:
Les Humanoides Associes
Gerry Webb
Dark They Were & Golden Eyed, St Annes Court, London W1
Selecciones Illustradas
Fershid Bharucha, 'Echo des Savanes'
Anthea Shackleton
Amra
Mick